GETTING

in the Spirit

Getting in the Spirit
Copyright 2014 by Erin Nicholas

All Rights Reserved.

This is a work of fiction. Names, characters, places, and incidents are the product of the author's imagination or are used fictitiously, and any resemblance to actual persons, living or dead, business establishments, events, or locales is entirely coincidental.

ISBN: 0986324515
ISBN-13: 9780986324512

Editor: Heidi Moore
Cover artist: Laron Glover

Digital formatting: Author E.M.S.

GETTING
in the Spirit

A SAPPHIRE FALLS NOVELLA

ERIN NICHOLAS

IT'S CHRISTMAS TIME IN

Sapphire Falls!

At least one good thing has come from Levi Spencer's car accident—it seems to have knocked some sense into him. He's ready to leave his wild Vegas playboy ways behind and become a new man. And he knows just the place to do it…his brother Joe's new hometown. He's never spent time in a place described as quaint or idyllic, and now he intends to revel in every charming, sweet thing he can find. Like the homegrown country girl his brother sets him up with for the Christmas formal.

Kate Leggot wants just one great Christmas. After a childhood without Christmas at all and three failed attempts to find the seasonal magic on her own, she agrees to spend the holiday with her friend Phoebe in Sapphire Falls. The Christmas-crazy town is a far cry from San Francisco and Kate quickly finds herself drawn into everything from the snow to the hot cocoa. And, of course, the sweet country boy Phoebe has set her up with for the formal. Looks like she's going to get everything she wanted—and more—under the tree this year.

A not-so-little mix-up, a hot kiss under the mistletoe and a candy cane or two later and December in Sapphire Falls has never been so hot.

This is a novella, about half the length of the novels in this series. Read only if you like fun, small town contemporary romances where they talk dirty and act even dirtier.

Dedication

To Heidi, who made this happen, like the goddess she is.

To my family who put up with Christmas music and Scentsy long before it was appropriate.

And to the inventor of the Starbucks white chocolate peppermint mocha…well done, my friend, well done.

One

"I fear for my cold, black soul."

Joe Spencer chuckled as he shifted his daughter to his other hip and pulled a packet of fruit snacks from the cupboard. His computer was on the kitchen table, his brother's image on screen.

"So dramatic, little brother."

"I'm serious. I'm fearing some Ghosts of Christmas Future if I fall asleep."

Joe shook his head. Levi was younger by eleven months and had never suffered from anything like guilt or contrition in all of his thirty two years.

Then again, Levi had also never had his brain banged around inside his skull in a could-have-been-fatal car accident.

"I believe there's only one Ghost of Christmas Future. There was also past and present," Joe said, fighting a smile.

"Whatever. Don't want any ghost visits at all." Levi sighed and leaned back against the pillows. "My fucking head hurts."

Joe frowned. "You're lucky that's all that hurts." Levi had driven his car into a ditch and flipped it twice. It was a miracle he was talking on the phone at the moment.

He looked like crap.

He was home now, on strict orders to rest and relax for several days. The headaches were getting better but were far from resolved. The doctors said that was to be expected. Joe had been by his bedside for the two days he'd been in the hospital and returned home to Sapphire Falls only yesterday.

"At least I'm out of the hospital. You know they gave me male nurses on purpose."

"Of course they did. They didn't want any of their female nurses shirking their duties to the other patients to take care of you."

Levi Spencer was one of the most, if not *the* most, eligible bachelors in Las Vegas. He was rich, for one thing, and couldn't help being charming any more than he could help his *gorgeous*—according to Joe's own wife—blue eyes, dark hair or I'm-trouble-and-you'll-love-every-minute-of-it grin.

"You're mostly bored," Joe said.

"None of my friends came to visit me in the hospital."

Joe sighed. He wasn't sure that Levi actually had any friends. He had a bunch of people who loved that he would always foot the bill.

"Did Juliet ever call you?" Joe asked of Levi's girlfriend.

"No." Levi paused. "And I don't care. See what I mean about the cold-black-soul thing?"

Joe tried not to grin. He couldn't completely disagree with Levi's assessment and he was happy that his little brother might have finally had a wakeup call.

"Hey, Levi, hold on a second." Joe tucked his daughter into her highchair and turned the computer so she could see Levi on the screen. "Kae, you talk to Uncle Levi for a few minutes. Tell him about going to grandma's house."

Kaelyn was ten months old and she'd babble long enough that Joe could get the laundry moved from the washing machine to the dryer.

Joe took his time as he heard his daughter's sweet voice regaling Levi with her big plans for the four-day stay with Phoebe's mom and dad while Joe and Phoebe headed to DC for some holiday parties. At least, that's what Joe assumed she was telling Levi. He grinned.

DC and its social life was part of Joe's job. It had gotten harder to be away from home since having Kaelyn, of course, but he'd been able to balance it all so far. While they loved their daughter to distraction, he and Phoebe were looking forward to the quick getaway. Joe was eternally grateful for his in-laws living right in Sapphire Falls and all of the friends they could count on to give them a hand.

Re-entering the kitchen, Joe swept Kaelyn up into his arms, grabbed her fruit snacks and the laptop and headed for the living room. They got settled on the couch and Joe was finally able to concentrate fully on his brother.

"I know you're bored, but you've got to listen to the doctors. The concussion is serious. You've got to lay off the partying, even if you're bored to death at home."

"Doc told me the same thing," Levi said. "The bastard."

Joe knew his brother didn't mean it. This accident, and the resulting head injury, had scared Levi. It helped that the doctor had taken Joe's advice and painted Levi a very grim picture of what could have been and what could still happen if he didn't take care of himself now. The concussion could have been a much more severe injury, one that could have had permanent consequences. That was no lie and barely an exaggeration.

"I need to turn over a new leaf." Levi was still leaning back in the bed, his eyes closed. His voice was low enough that Joe reached for the volume on his computer.

"I agree," Joe said simply.

Joe knew all about Levi's lifestyle. He'd been living a very similar one only four years ago. Before he'd come to Sapphire Falls and met Phoebe. He'd had no idea exactly how much his life really was going to change, and he loved every single bit of it.

The scent of fruit hit him and he looked down at Kaelyn, perched in his lap, happily eating her snack. Joe smiled at her and she returned the grin. His heart clenched so hard that he couldn't breathe for a moment.

Levi could use a huge dose of what Joe had. He didn't know what he was missing.

And Joe wanted him to know. Levi might squander money, might get easily bored with women and might have a slightly crooked moral compass, but he was Joe's brother and Joe loved him. He wanted him happy. He wanted him fulfilled. He wanted him not dead in a ditch.

It wasn't like Joe hadn't tried giving advice, but Levi had a hard head.

Which was fortunate when he plowed his car into ditches.

"Maybe you should come hang out in Sapphire Falls for a while," Joe said, still looking at his daughter. She was the spitting image of her mother—bright red curls, huge grin and sparkly personality. Joe had never known he could love anyone as much as he loved his wife and daughter. He would do anything to keep them safe and happy. He always put them before anything he wanted for himself.

Levi needed that—something that was more important to him than himself. Levi was an incredibly intelligent guy. Joe had suspected for a long time that Levi's problem was mostly that he had no challenges, nothing to keep his attention or engage his mind for longer than about fifteen minutes. Levi was like a big kid who had never been given any rules and had an unlimited allowance at his disposal. He jumped from one thing, one party, one woman, to another like he was flipping channels on a television, unable to find anything worth watching for long.

Levi sat up and looked into the screen. "Seriously? You want me to come to Sapphire Falls?"

"Yes," Joe said firmly. "It's the holidays. The last place you need to be is in Vegas with all the parties and stuff." Levi would never be able to resist all of that. "Come stay with us. Phoebe will fuss over you, you can kick back and eat homemade everything. You can sleep late and relax. It's exactly what you need."

The sleepy little town of Sapphire Falls, population twelve hundred and twenty one, was the exact opposite of Levi's pace. He loved the lights, noise and over-the-top feeling in Vegas. He and Joe had literally been raised amongst the neon and craziness so for years they'd both accepted it as normal. Joe had, fortunately, landed in Sapphire Falls and now couldn't imagine living anywhere that didn't have things like the annual town festival and the strawberry festival and the winter festival. They were really into festivals. But the flashiest Sapphire Falls got was with the fireworks at…well, all of the festivals…and the Christmas tree lighting in the town square.

"Are you sure that would be okay?" Levi asked.

It occurred to Joe that he'd never invited Levi to Sapphire Falls. He got a kick out of sending photos and texts or emails about the town because he knew that Levi would laugh and shake his head and think Joe was making half of the stuff up. But the senior citizens really did teach the kindergartners to ballroom dance, and they really did have a pumpkin festival, complete with a pumpkin-pie-eating contest, and they really did have music playing softly overhead in the downtown area at all times.

Sometimes it was Frank Sinatra, sometimes it was fifties rock and roll, sometimes it was old country—Johnny Cash and company—sometimes it was instrumental.

Now that it was the holidays, the seemingly constant festive feel in Sapphire Falls had been kicked up another notch. They'd had a cocoa tasting in the square last week. The square had been completely decked out and there was a horse-drawn sleigh driving around town giving people rides. And the music was now twenty-four seven Christmas carols. Of course.

"I want you here for Christmas," Joe said. Levi needed to get out of Vegas, but it was also because he was Joe's brother. Joe had never realized all he'd been missing not having a close family. Now that he had Phoebe and Kaelyn and all of Phoebe's family—more than twenty-five percent of the town—and their friends, Joe couldn't imagine ever being where Levi was right now.

Joe and Levi's family wasn't traditional in really any sense. Their grandfather and father headed up Spencer Enterprises and owned several casinos in the US. Their primary offices were in Vegas and, yes, Joe and Levi had more or less grown up in casinos.

Their childhoods—raised by two parents who were together for seemingly every reason but love—surrounded by scantily clad women, neon and people throwing money around, whether they could afford it or not, had been…interesting.

Up until four years ago, Joe had embraced it all. It was fun to live hard with no consequences. Two things that passed through the male genes in the Spencer family was an absolute love for all things excessive and the lack of shame.

They could have been poster children for the seven deadly sins.

Then Joe had awakened in a bed in a hotel room in a city with no recollection of how he'd gotten there or even where *there* was for several long, frightening minutes. He'd decided then and there to change his life.

Levi had *finally* hit rock bottom, and Joe knew exactly what his brother needed.

"I could probably come spend a few days," Levi said.

Joe grinned. He could tell his brother liked the idea but didn't want to show how much it meant to him.

"Sapphire Falls is the perfect idea," Joe said. The small town he now considered home had saved him in every way a man could be saved. "Stay all the way through New Year's. Recover, relax. You won't believe how real people spend Christmas, man. It's like every Christmas card, story, song or movie you've ever seen or heard."

Christmas was magical in Sapphire Falls. It was perfect and nothing could heal a black, cold soul like Christmas in the country.

Christmas with his family had consisted of a house full of people that Joe didn't even know, walking in on his father screwing some lady Joe had never seen before on the couch in the den, his mother kissing some guy he'd never seen before under the mistletoe and everyone getting drunk and stupid.

Real keepsake memories there.

"I think I'll stay for a year."

Joe was jerked away from his memories of Christmas past. "What?" He focused on Levi.

His brother was looking more alert than he'd been in days. He was even smiling. Joe blinked.

"Yeah, why not?" Levi said. "The doctor says I need to quit drinking, not stay up all night and generally stop doing everything I do right now. There's nothing to stay up all night for in Sapphire Falls, is there?"

Part of Joe wanted to protest that, but it was true that the last time he'd stayed up all night in Sapphire Falls he'd been making love to Phoebe all night. And they'd slept past noon the next day.

Yeah, Sapphire Falls would be a good place to change most of Levi's bad habits, if for no other reason than because there would be far fewer opportunities in Sapphire Falls to partake in those habits.

Levi wouldn't even be able to satisfy his addiction to Butterfingers after ten p.m. on weeknights.

"A year, huh?" Joe asked. That was a long time.

"It's going to take more than a couple of weeks at Christmas to save me," Levi said. "This will be better than rehab. Good healthy food, nice people, relaxed pace, nice women."

Ah, women.

"So you're giving up drinking and partying and junk food but not women?" Joe asked.

His brother needed his help. But the women in his new hometown did *not* need Joe letting Levi loose on them.

Levi actually chuckled at Joe's question. "Give up women? I think that's a little drastic."

Right.

"Besides, I think it would be even better for me to date a nice country girl than it would be to give women up entirely."

"A nice country girl," Joe repeated. He had a bad feeling about this.

"A nice girl like Phoebe."

Joe was aware that Levi was intrigued by Joe's wife. Phoebe had that effect on people. But she was so unlike the women Levi was used to hanging out with. She was what-you-see-is-what-you-get. She didn't try to impress Joe. She dressed nicely but was never overdone. She was sweet and kind and caring, but she would always be in-your-face honest if you pissed her off. She was...amazing.

There were no other women in the world like Phoebe. And she was all Joe's.

But there were other women in Sapphire Falls that could teach Levi a thing or two about how to treat a lady, who wouldn't be bowled over by his money or his designer labels, who he would have to actually work to impress.

That might be very good for him, come to think of it.

"There's got to be a couple of girls who would be able to teach me about a slow-moving, sweet, monogamous relationship," Levi said.

Joe blinked at him again.

"What?" Levi asked.

"I wasn't aware that you knew the word monogamous."

"Ha, ha."

But Joe had been serious.

"Well, there is a Christmas formal coming up."

"A *formal?*" Levi asked, using the word formal sarcastically.

Joe nodded. "Yep. Formal dresses, tuxes, the whole bit." It was new and definitely fancier than the little town was used to, but everyone was getting into the idea of dressing up and dancing the night away. The school's gymnasium was slowly being transformed into a winter wonderland now that school was out for the holiday break.

"So you can set me up?" Levi asked. "I need a nice girl who can teach me to be a gentleman and who will keep me out of trouble. Introduce me to one of Phoebe's friends. Or a cousin."

Joe chuckled, going through the women he knew in Sapphire Falls that might be able to handle Levi. Sure, a nice girl would be good for Levi in some ways, but Joe refused to have Levi blow into town, make some sweet girl fall for him and then leave a broken heart behind. A broken heart that would blame Joe.

So he wasn't going to set Levi up with any of the really nice girls he knew.

He thought about Phoebe's closest friends.

Lauren would be able to handle Levi for sure. She was a city girl who had turned country. She'd be able to see Levi coming from a mile away and would have him wrapped around her finger before Levi even used all his lines on her.

But Lauren was married to Travis Bennett, and there was no way Travis would let Levi Spencer anywhere near Lauren. Travis would also see Levi coming a mile away.

There was Phoebe's best friend Adrianne. She would also be quite able to handle Levi. Adrianne was sweeter than Lauren and wouldn't be quite as in-his-face with Levi, but she would absolutely be able to keep him in line.

Of course, Adrianne was married to Mason Riley, one of Joe's bosses, and they had two kids now—incredibly bright, curious little boys only a year apart who loved to dig in the dirt and get into anything and everything they could. Adrianne was running from sunup to sundown, keeping up with them as they put things in the microwave that didn't belong in the microwave and brought animals and bugs and reptiles into her house as pets.

Then he thought about Phoebe's other close friend. The four women were kind of an unlikely bunch. They'd been brought together by various, strange circumstances for sure. But the friendship had evolved through the three romances—Adrianne's, Phoebe's and Lauren's—and they never missed their weekly margarita meeting.

Hailey Conner was the only one who was still single. And Hailey could most definitely handle Levi. Hailey was the Mayor of Sapphire Falls. A hometown girl who had always been popular, sort-of liked and sort-of feared as gorgeous, confident, mean girls always were. Hailey had gotten progressively less mean over the years. To hear Phoebe tell stories from high school, Hailey had never met a person or a situation she couldn't manipulate to her own purposes. Still, Joe knew his wife actually liked Hailey now. As much as that surprised her.

Hailey was actually very much Levi's type. She was one of maybe half a dozen women in town who could tell the difference between Prada and a knock-off. She always looked amazing. She had a confident sensuality that had many men enamored. But she was still a country girl at heart. She'd spent her life in Sapphire Falls and loved her hometown more than anything. She was, actually, a very good mayor.

Hailey was the perfect woman to set Levi up with. She could introduce him to small-town life, she would demand he treat her well, would keep him in line, but she wouldn't fall for all of his charming bullshit.

"You know what?" Joe said. "I think I have the perfect woman for you."

"Yeah? Great. I'll be there day after tomorrow."

Joe nodded. "I'll set it up for you two to meet that night." Probably the sooner someone was keeping track of Levi, the better.

"Great." Levi actually looked happy. That was really nice to see.

Joe smiled. Then he remembered a not-so-tiny detail. "Shit. Phoebe and I won't be here."

"When?"

"In two days. We're heading to DC for some holiday get-togethers. But with travel and everything we'll be gone about four days."

"That's okay. If it's okay with you, I'll come anyway and get settled," Levi said. "I'll use the guest room through the holidays, but then I'll look for something to buy."

Levi definitely had the money to simply plunk a wad of cash down on a house in Sapphire Falls that he intended to use for his year of *rehab*. "Yes, that's fine, of course. I'll be sure the fridge has something in it."

"Don't worry about anything," Levi said. "I'm a big boy with a massive credit limit. And I need to get to know my new neighbors, right? I'll get some groceries, check out the local eating establishments. It will be fine."

Joe laughed. "Checking out the local eating establishments won't take long. You can get a sandwich at Scott's Sweets, a burger or wings at the Come Again, or breakfast, lunch and dinner at Dottie's, the diner downtown."

Levi grinned. "Can't wait."

Joe wondered for a moment if leaving and having Levi come to town and be on his own for a few days was a good idea.

But really, what could happen?

Besides, he'd fill Hailey in and be sure she was keeping an eye on him.

"I am boycotting all things peppermint, red, green and joyful."

Phoebe Spencer laughed. "You don't mean that."

"Oh, but I do. I'm going to get Chinese takeout and do a Netflix marathon of Marvel comic movies."

Phoebe was almost afraid to ask. "Why Marvel comic movies?"

"I can't watch TV without running into Christmas movies and specials, so I have to stick with Netflix where I can control what's on. Marvel because there are no Christmas themes and they are full of hot guys doing the right thing for the greater good. Unlike real-life human men."

Phoebe grimaced and was glad she wasn't skyping with Kate so her friend couldn't see her. "I'm sorry you're so bummed out."

"Christmas just kind of sucks for me. Always has."

Kate Leggot was twenty-nine and lived in San Francisco. She had never even been to Nebraska, not to mention tiny little Sapphire Falls. She was gorgeous, sophisticated and intelligent. She was an environmental engineer who was studying a number of climate change issues that required her to travel to DC to meet and educate politicians. Phoebe didn't understand everything Kate was doing, but she was used to that being friends with brilliant scientists like Mason and Lauren. Phoebe's husband, Joe, worked for Innovative Agricultural Solutions, a company that was developing new cutting-edge farming techniques for use in third-world countries and sustainable farming for poorer areas of the US. Phoebe and Kate had ended up seated next to one another at a fund-raising dinner in DC about a year ago and had instantly hit it off. They had very little in common and yet enjoyed each other's company immensely.

"Christmas is my favorite," Phoebe said. She grabbed a bag of diapers from the shelf and added it to her shopping cart. "Why don't you like it?"

Kate sighed. "My mom never liked Christmas, so we never celebrated when I was a kid."

"You never had Christmas as a kid?" Phoebe asked. "That's terrible."

Kate laughed softly. "Well, I didn't know what I was missing for a long time. But obviously as I got older it was pretty hard to miss all around me, all the kids talking about it at school and stuff."

"I'm sure." Phoebe knew, of course, that Christmas was not celebrated by everyone, but she'd grown up in Sapphire Falls. It was a wonderful, accepting place but it was not a very diverse place. Everyone in Sapphire Falls celebrated Christmas. "Is your family Jewish?" That hadn't even occurred to her. That was terrible.

"No," Kate said. "My mom just hates Christmas. So we left for Hawaii every year before Thanksgiving and didn't come back until well after the New Year."

"Mid-November to mid-January in Hawaii?" Phoebe asked with a laugh. "You poor thing."

"Yeah, I know it sounds great. But Hawaii isn't Christmasy, you know?"

"Honey, you live in California. It's not like you guys sing "Let It Snow" right?"

Kate sighed. "I know. I guess I always wished that I had a grandmother or aunt or something that lived somewhere that it snowed. I used to watch those Christmas specials on TV and think that Christmas was so much cooler for people who had snow."

Phoebe snorted. "It's definitely cooler."

Kate actually laughed softly at that. "For years, I begged my parents to go skiing or something instead of to Hawaii. Even if we didn't do Christmas, I just wanted snow. But they never went for that idea."

"Wow. Your parents had money?" Phoebe asked, adding eggs to her cart and then taking them back out. She and Joe were going to be gone for four days. She should stick with non-perishables for now. They'd have to eat cereal for breakfast in the morning. She did grab milk though. Kaelyn would need milk tonight and tomorrow morning.

"My parents had—have—lots of money."

"Now that you say that, I can see it. You have that sophisticated I-ride-in-limos air about you," Phoebe said.

"I'm not going to ask if that's a good thing."

"It's not good or bad. Joe grew up with money and limos too," Phoebe said. "I grew up with pickup trucks. Pros and cons to both."

"I guess." Kate sighed.

"So you hate Christmas because you never got to have snow? Surely you've traveled to places with snow?" Phoebe asked, adding coffee to her cart. She also grabbed a box of wheat flakes that she knew she should eat, pushed the cart about three feet, then backed up and exchanged the wheat flakes for the sugary fruity O's she loved. Next time she'd buy the healthy cereal. Or maybe the time after that.

"I have and I love it," Kate said.

Phoebe shook her head. "Try scooping it out of your driveway and scraping your windshield every morning for about four months, you'll get over it."

"Isn't that what you have that gorgeous, hunky husband for?" Kate teased.

Phoebe grinned. "Well, yeah, *now*. But I had to teach him to scrape and shovel. He grew up in Vegas."

And he'd been darned cute the first time he'd tried to maneuver the snow blower. Phoebe grinned, remembering him banging into the house, proclaiming he was about to die of frost bite if she didn't warm him up immediately. They'd been naked and very, very warm within minutes.

"So get on a plane and go somewhere with snow," Phoebe said. "If that's all you need to feel better about the best holiday all year, then that's easy."

"Oh, it's not just the Hawaii and snow thing," Kate said. "The past three Christmases, I've had boyfriend issues. This year, I'm staying inside. Away from Christmas and guys and any thoughts of combining the two. I'm going to hunker down with junk food and Marvel until New Year's is past. Then I'm going to get up, go back to my regular routine and forget there even was a Christmas this year."

"You can't do that," Phoebe protested. She loved Christmas. Everything about it. And Sapphire Falls did Christmas big. It was like every holiday movie, song or story ever told. She hated the idea her friend would be down on Christmas.

"I can," Kate assured her. "I'll be okay."

"Tell me about these guys that have ruined Christmas for you."

Kate sighed. "Three years ago, I caught my boyfriend kissing one of the girls I work with at our Christmas party. Cliché, I know, but it hurt."

"Of course it did," Phoebe said sympathetically.

"The next year, my boyfriend dumped me on Christmas Day. We were supposed to have dinner with his family, and at the last minute, he decided that he wasn't serious enough about me to introduce me to his parents. We'd been dating exclusively for six months at that point. I decided if he wasn't serious by then, he wouldn't be serious."

"I think that was a good choice." Phoebe mentally thanked Heaven for Joe. She'd found the man of her dreams and she was never going to have to be back out there dating ever again.

"And then last year, my boyfriend stole two of my credit cards and my car. On Christmas Eve."

Phoebe gasped. The two women in the aisle with her—one of them the mother of one of Phoebe's students and the other her aunt Karen—both looked over. She gave them a smile and a wave.

"Wow, honey, you have had a rough few Christmases."

"I've never had a good Christmas." Kate sounded totally dejected. "I can't handle watching it all happen around me. People are walking along the sidewalks, holding hands, picking out gifts. I turn on the TV and it's all these movies about falling in love at Christmas. I turn on the radio and it's all about it being cold outside—which it's not here—and how people are rocking around the Christmas tree. While I'm here alone wishing I could be rocking *under* the Christmas tree. I can't take it."

Phoebe snorted. "You have a Christmas tree fantasy?"

"I do," Kate said with feeling. "I really do. The room's dark, the only lights on are from the fireplace and the lights on the tree…" She trailed off. "But I don't even have a fireplace."

Phoebe stopped with a bunch of bananas in hand. "Tell me you have a tree, Kate," she said. "Please tell me you have a tree."

"Nope. No tree. I told you, no Christmas here this year."

Well, that was unacceptable.

"You need to go buy a plane ticket," Phoebe decided. "I have snow, a tree, a fireplace and…" She thought fast. She couldn't let this sweet woman spend the holiday alone ignoring that there even was a holiday. What Kate needed was Sapphire Falls. No one could *not* be in the Christmas spirit in Sapphire Falls. "And I have a nice, sweet, cute country boy to make you feel all better."

Her wheels were turning. She needed to set Kate up with someone. Someone nice. Someone who would be a gentleman. Someone who could give her a good romantic Christmas memory to erase all the bad ones.

It wouldn't have to be true love. A fun holiday fling would be perfect.

"You do?" Kate asked. "Are you kidding?"

Phoebe was *really* glad they weren't on Skype where Kate might be able to tell that Phoebe was making this up as she went. "Yes, of course. You can't breathe the air or drink the water here without getting in the Christmas spirit," Phoebe said. "And I was wondering what to get you as a gift."

Kate laughed. "You're giving me a sweet country boy as a Christmas gift?"

"I'm giving you one perfect Christmas. We have it all here, honey. You'll feel like you stepped into a movie."

Who was she going to set Kate up with though? She thought through the single guys in town.

"You're going to make a guy take me out for Christmas?"

"Oh, yeah," Phoebe scoffed. "What a hardship. I bring a beautiful, classy, smart, sweet girl to town and ask him to take her to the Christmas formal. I'm sure he'll never forgive me."

"Well…"

Phoebe detected a definite note of interest. Kate wasn't shooting her down anyway.

"I do love snow. So much. And I've never been to a small town at Christmas."

"I'm telling you, it's like falling into the North Pole here," Phoebe said. She unloaded her cart onto the conveyor belt at the checkout and smiled at the cashier. She'd had Tiffany in class last year.

"So who's the guy?" Kate finally asked.

Yes, who indeed? The most eligible bachelors in town forever had been the Bennett boys, but Travis was definitely no longer single, and TJ was way too grumpy to give a girl a nice sweet Christmas.

Which left…

Phoebe felt her smile spread. He was perfect. He was sweet, cute and romantic but wouldn't take it too seriously if Phoebe told him her friend was in town for only a few days and for the formal. Hell, he'd probably love to romance Kate, have a fling and then say goodbye.

"His name is Tucker Bennett," Phoebe told her.

She heard Kate take a deep breath. Phoebe held her breath, waiting for Kate's decision.

"I can be there in a couple of days."

Phoebe breathed and grinned. "Awesome. This will be so fun. We can make cookies and go for a sleigh ride and—*dammit.*"

Tiffany looked up, startled.

"What?" Kate asked.

Phoebe swiped her debit card through the machine and sighed. "We're going to be out of town for the next few days. DC parties." She frowned. "Hey, why aren't you going to DC to the parties?"

"I backed out," Kate said. "Told my boss that the holidays bring up lots of negative emotions and I couldn't handle the parties. He and his wife are going. He's actually thrilled."

Phoebe hated the idea of Kate staying in California. She was afraid if Kate got her takeout and got the movie marathon going there would be no getting her out of her apartment, not to mention on a plane. "Come anyway. I can give you directions to the house. We leave a key under the ceramic frog next to the porch." She had no problem saying that out loud in the middle of the grocery store. The few people in Sapphire Falls who did lock their doors had similar ceramic creatures near their porches sitting on their spare keys. "You can come, make yourself at home, enjoy the tree and fireplace. You can watch Netflix here. We'll be home in a few days and it will all be good."

Kate was quiet for a long moment.

Phoebe nodded when Hunter, the kid who was bagging groceries, asked if she wanted him to carry her bags to the car.

She was opening her trunk for Hunter when Kate finally said, "That sounds really nice."

"Awesome. This is going to be the best Christmas, I promise."

Kate laughed. "Well, it wouldn't take much."

Two

If a hundred of Santa's elves had eaten too many Christmas cookies and thrown up all over, the town square in Sapphire Falls would have been the result.

Levi sat behind the wheel of his rented Maserati coup and stared.

There were four Christmas trees, one on each corner of the square, fully decorated. There was a gingerbread house—big enough that three or four young kids could fit inside. There was a life-sized sleigh. At least a dozen five-foot plastic candy canes lined the sidewalk. Plastic ornaments in various shapes, all about the size of car tires, hung from the branches of the non-evergreen trees in the square. A gazebo with a huge throne-like chair and a banner that read *Welcome to Sapphire Falls, Santa* occupied the center of the square. And, no shit, there was a penned-in area next to one of the trees that had two real, living, breathing reindeer munching on hay.

As if even Mother Nature was conspiring for a perfect Christmas scene, there was also a slight dusting of powdery white snow over everything.

"Holy sleigh bells."

He'd fallen into a fricking Christmas card.

Just like Joe had said.

His brother had used words like idyllic and quaint to describe the place, and he'd sent photos of town events that Levi had, in all honesty, thought were fake. Levi knew it was a small country town that prided itself on its welcoming, homey feel. But…wow.

He parked the car in front of the grocery store and got out. It wasn't hard to find the businesses in Sapphire Falls. They were all clustered around the square. A block away from the square in any direction took you into residential areas. The one exception was south of the square. A block off of the grassy area was the main highway that went past Sapphire Falls, and along the highway was a gas station, the Come Again bar and the little strip mall area that housed several local businesses, including a homemade furniture shop, a card and stationary shop and Scott's Sweets, a candy shop and bakery.

Overhead, Levi heard the soft strains of Silver Bells and he glanced up. He couldn't find where they'd hidden the speakers, but he did see that there were indeed silver bells hanging from the lamp posts that dotted the street in both directions.

There was no way the Ghost of Christmas Future would mess with him here. Levi felt a huge grin stretch across his face. Simply breathing the air here was making him a better person. He didn't even mind the nearly thirty degree drop in temperature or the fact he could see his breath. It was refreshing. Exactly what he needed. Sweet beyond description.

There was mistletoe around here somewhere. He just knew it.

Grinning like a damned idiot, Levi headed into the store and grabbed shampoo and the other toiletries he hated to pack and headed to pay. He was aware that he was drawing attention from the other shoppers and store employees and he gave them all his most sincere smiles. He had to behave here. This was Joe's hometown. No hitting on the cute girl shopping in aisle three. No flirting with the beautiful forty-something buying apples. No making the young—very young—cashier blush.

Back in his car, he started toward Joe's place. He had instructions printed off from Joe's email. He knew Joe and Phoebe lived out in the country outside of town, and Levi couldn't wait to see this. Sapphire Falls *was* the country as far as Levi was concerned.

He'd only gotten about a mile outside of town and turned onto the dirt road when he realized that his brother no longer drove a sports car, not because he'd matured and no longer put his self-worth in material things, but because a low-slung coupe was impractical on roads that were gravel and mud and snow.

Creeping along, praying as he went that he wouldn't get stuck out here where he had no one to call and no idea how exactly to get to Joe's on foot, Levi made it another mile before there was another road. He glanced at the directions in his lap. He didn't dare actually stop the car for fear of not getting it going again so he kept moving as he read the tiny type. Why hadn't he increased the font size? He was supposed to go another hundred yards and he'd find Joe's driveway.

One hundred yards later there was another dirt road. This was narrower, bordered on both sides by big old trees and with two deep ruts running from the road up to the house he could see in the distance. Deep ruts that were obviously caused by truck tires.

Awesome.

He turned in, grimacing as he heard and felt the crusty snow underneath dragging along the bottom of the car.

He finally made it to the house, pulled over onto a flat slab of cement beside the garage and turned off the ignition. Thank goodness.

At least, he hoped this was Joe's place. And he hoped that his brother's truck was here and that they'd left the keys.

The front door key was under the ceramic frog as Joe had said it would be, and a minute later, Levi let himself into the farm house with his suitcase and grocery sack.

He let the bags fall as he took in a big lungful of air. The house smelled amazing. It was neat and homey. There were no Christmas decorations up yet, but it was only the twentieth and Joe and Phoebe were supposed to be home on the twenty-second. They'd all decorate together. Levi felt a surge of happiness. Pure, unadulterated happiness. It had nothing to do with a winning poker hand or a shot of alcohol or a woman's cleavage. It was about feeling at home, warm, safe, cared about.

Levi Spencer would never ever admit it to anyone, ever, but when Joe had invited him to Sapphire Falls, Levi had felt his heart actually swell. The organ he'd thought shriveled like a raisin long ago had thumped in his chest, reminding him that it was there and working.

Joe and Phoebe were the only people in the entire world that Levi could say with absolute certainty cared about him.

Joe's invitation had meant more to Levi than he'd realized. He was even a little choked up.

If that wasn't the damnedest thing, he didn't know what was.

He hauled his bags up the stairs to the guest room. He was even more shocked when the choked-up feeling increased when he passed his niece's bedroom. The scent of baby powder and the sight of a purple stuffed elephant sitting on the seat of the rocking chair made his cold, dead heart thump again.

Damn.

Who knew he was a big pile of mush underneath the Rolex and Armani?

It had to be the concussion. He must have jarred some feeling loose when he'd banged his skull into the car window.

The guest room was the third door on the right. Levi pushed the door open and threw his bag on the bed. Then he turned a full circle. The quilt on the bed was…a quilt. He had never slept under an actual quilt in his life. Levi would put good money on the fact someone Phoebe was related to had made the thing. The bed was a four-poster queen.

The bedroom floor was refinished wood with a huge woven rug on top to keep it from being cold. There were two big windows in the west and north walls covered in simple cotton curtains that matched the maroon color in the quilt. There was an overstuffed reading chair in the corner, an armoire on one wall, and the remaining wall held a collection of black-and-white photographs that were clearly of Phoebe's family over the generations on the front porch of this very house.

Again, Levi felt something that could have been emotions clogging his throat.

For fuck's sake. It was like a dam had broken open. He needed to get a handle on things. He couldn't be all weepy and sentimental. Joe would send him for further medical work-up for sure.

Levi riffled through his bag, planning to change into something more Sapphire Falls appropriate. He was heading to the Come Again. Not because he needed a drink—even though he *so* needed a drink—but because that was where he was meeting his date for the Christmas formal. The woman who was going to keep him from being a complete and total asshole who thought of women for only one thing. Okay, two things—sex and his ego.

Surely recognizing that he was a womanizing ass was a step in the right direction.

He pulled out his phone and thumbed through to the message from Joe sent earlier that day.

She'll meet you at the Come Again at eight. Built blonde in a red dress. You won't be able to miss her.

Built blonde. Red dress. This was already a good idea.

Finding nothing quite right for the tiny bar in the tiny town in his bag, Levi headed for the master bedroom. He dug through a dresser drawer and found a pair of blue jeans and a black cotton T-shirt. In the closet, he found a pair of black Oxford shoes. The leather was soft and they obviously weren't new, but it was those or a pair of brown work boots.

He was going to have to ask Joe about those boots. Joe Spencer was wearing boots? To do what? Muck out the stalls in his barn?

Levi chuckled to himself, but as he turned to exit the room, he glanced out the window. This one faced east and, sure enough, there was a barn in the distance.

For a second, Levi wondered what he'd gotten into.

Changing your life around before the ghosts get to you.

It was an analogy. He didn't really think ghosts were coming to bring him a message about changing his life. He did, however, fully expect to have a stocking full of coal on Christmas morning.

Half an hour later, he walked into the Come Again bar in tiny Sapphire Falls, Nebraska, and thought maybe the Ghost of Christmas Present wasn't such a bad guy.

The built blonde in the red dress sitting at the bar was exquisite.

It had been clear within three seconds of stepping into the Come Again that Kate was overdressed. But a night out at the pubs in her neighborhood meant fitted red dresses, a sexy twist to her hair and full make up.

At the Come Again, the dress code was clearly denim, cotton and more denim.

Kate pressed her lips together and rubbed as she lifted her glass of wine, trying to blot some of her lipstick off. None of the other women were wearing anything more than cherry lip balm.

She sipped and then set her glass down with surprisingly steady hands. It wasn't nerves about the date. Phoebe had set it up, and Kate knew Phoebe. This was about Kate having a nice Christmas. The guy would be great. Funny, sweet, interested in helping her have a nice time. Her antsy feelings were about being the center of attention in a room full of strangers. She could hardly miss the blatant stares from all of the other patrons. Everyone was watching her with such open curiosity she almost laughed. She had no trouble being alone. Even drinking alone. But she felt compelled to engage them all in conversation for some reason. Even stranger was the realization that she would have nothing in common with any of these people.

What was she going to talk to her *date* about? He was a Sapphire Falls boy born and raised. What was his name again? Oh God, she couldn't even remember his name. It was some country-boy name. Trent? Trey? Tate? She wrinkled her nose. Tate was a country *club* boy's name. She pulled her phone from her purse and opened her text messages.

"Tucker Bennett."

Tucker. That was definitely a country-boy's name. Kate smiled. Not having anything in common with him could only be a good thing. She wanted to get away from her life for a while.

Phoebe had also included, *"Dark hair, blue eyes, killer smile."*

Kate had texted back asking what he'd be wearing. Phoebe's answer had made her laugh.

"One thousand percent sure he'll be wearing blue jeans and a T-shirt."

That was clearly a good bet, Kate thought, sipping her wine and covertly checking the room out. Every guy in the room was in blue jeans and the split between cotton T-shirts and cotton plaid shirts was about fifty-fifty.

There was a pool game going in the corner, music that she didn't recognize other than to know it was country played from the jukebox and couples were moving around the dance floor in a coordinated pattern. She knew that was a two-step. She did watch movies and TV after all.

"Christmas just became my favorite holiday."

Kate felt goose bumps dance down her spine at the rich, deep voice behind her. She swallowed her mouthful of wine and then turned slowly on the stool. She wanted to savor this moment. This was the first step toward her perfect, magical Christmas.

Tucker Bennett was gorgeous.

That was Kate's first thought. Phoebe had said cute. She'd said he was a nice guy. She had mentioned the killer smile and blue eyes, but she had failed to warn Kate that she wouldn't be able to breathe when she actually met Tucker's gaze directly.

Holy jingle bells. This was gonna be good.

"Hi," she said, trying to decide if she sounded sexy breathless or crazy breathless.

Obviously, Phoebe had told him she would be his date for the Christmas formal and Tucker would know she was from out of town, especially considering he probably knew every single person in Sapphire Falls and their grandmother. But she couldn't be all gaga and pathetic. She wanted a movie-worthy Christmas, but she couldn't fall all over Tucker. He'd signed on to be her date, not the savior of everything Christmas thus far in her life.

She needed to get a grip.

"Joe is a really, really good guy," Tucker said.

She smiled. That sounded positive. And she couldn't disagree. Tucker was probably a friend of Joe's, and Phoebe had probably gotten Joe to talk him into this. Kate wondered briefly what Phoebe had told Joe and what Joe had shared with Tucker.

But it didn't matter. He was here now and he was…magnificent.

She found herself staring at his mouth.

Crap.

She pulled her gaze back to his with a surprising amount of effort required. She couldn't throw herself at this guy. He was a nice small-town guy doing a favor for a friend of a friend. Guys in sweet little towns didn't do hot hook ups with girls they didn't know. Hell, Tucker had probably known every girl he'd ever taken out since kindergarten.

Besides, she wasn't a hook-up kind of girl. She liked sex, but she needed more than two sentences to get out of her panties.

"I'm sure hoping there's mistletoe around here somewhere."

Okay, maybe three sentences. Or him just standing there smiling at her.

Oh boy, this might be a problem. Or not. She did have that Christmas tree fantasy after all. She'd been planning on having a sweet, romantic Christmas with a nice guy who was fun but had no chance of breaking her heart because the expectations were clear and simple.

But she could probably squeeze in some hot sex by Christmas tree light with Tucker.

Phoebe and Joe didn't have their tree up yet. She'd found the house a few hours ago and had unpacked, showered and gotten dressed before coming back to town. But maybe Tucker had his tree up.

As she continued to stare at him, her gaze dipping to his mouth over and over. His smile was relaxed and he stepped forward, the look in his eyes more intent than playful now. "Or maybe we can skip the mistletoe altogether."

She was acting like an idiot.

She was vaguely aware of the fact, but she couldn't seem to stop.

She'd dated good-looking guys before. She'd dated good-looking guys who knew they were good looking before. But there was something about Tucker. It wasn't only his looks. It was the way he was focused on her, fully concentrated, as if the world around them didn't exist. It was the way he moved into her personal space without hesitation, or permission, like he belonged there. It was the way he met and held her gaze. The way he blatantly studied her—but not her body, not her breasts, not her legs—her face.

It should have been unnerving. She would have expected it to be unnerving. But it was…tempting.

She felt like he was drawing her in, pulling her closer, relaxing her and opening her up.

She wanted to cuddle close, take a long, deep whiff of his scent, feel his warmth and strength against her and…yes, take off her clothes.

"This is going to be a problem," he said softly, for her ears only.

She cleared her throat and finally forced words out. "What is?"

"The way you're looking at me. I was under the impression that we were going to be having hot cocoa together."

She shook her head, trying not to make hot cocoa and chocolaty melted marshmallows dirty. And failing. "What's that mean?"

"Hot cocoa is warm and comforting and sweet."

"Okay," she said slowly, not following.

"The way you're looking at me is like spiked hot apple cider."

Kate felt herself grin at the comparison. And he wasn't wrong. There wasn't anything particularly comforting or sweet about the things she was feeling.

Damn, she was ruining this. She was the one who wanted sweet and comforting. If she wanted hot sex and white wine, she could have stayed in San Francisco. She knew a number of guys who would have gone for that. "I'm sorry."

"Don't be sorry." There was a gruffness to his voice that made those goose bumps pop up again.

She leaned back. She was sending the wrong message. Phoebe knew she wanted a *date*. She wanted to spend time with a nice guy who was willing to indulge her need for some Christmas nostalgia. And now she was looking at him like she'd like to cover him in eggnog and then lick it all up.

Kate squeezed her thighs together. *Don't be the frisky city girl who comes to town for a quickie*, she told herself. *Be nice, be sweet, let him romance you. That's what you want.*

"Do you have a tree up yet at your place?" she asked. Sure, she kind of wanted to get naughty under the evergreen branches, but she also really loved Christmas trees. Her family had never had Christmas trees. For a while, she'd put one up in her apartment, but she'd consciously forgone that tradition last year, and it hadn't even occurred to her this year.

Tucker studied her for a long moment and then leaned back. "Not yet," he admitted. "But if you want a Christmas tree, I can find you a Christmas tree. What do you say to some cocoa after all?"

She nodded. "I'd like that." Cocoa. Not spiked hot cider. She was here for *cocoa*.

He stepped back and offered his hand to help her off the stool. She took it and felt all of her girl parts swoon.

Crap, she was in trouble.

Maybe Phoebe didn't realize Tucker was this potent, but he was not what Kate had been expecting. Or wanting. She wanted a nice guy. Someone who could make her laugh, someone who would hold her hand. Not someone who made her feel itchy and hot.

They stepped outside a moment later and Kate sucked in a quick breath. She was grateful for the heat he generated now. It was chilly. More than chilly. It was fricking cold. Especially compared to California.

Phoebe had left a long coat draped over one of the dining room chairs with a note that said Kate was to wear it, along with the scarf, gloves and hat in the pockets. She known that the California girl wouldn't have any winter clothes.

Kate pulled the long white coat closed in front and buttoned it up, then looped the bright red scarf around her neck and pulled the matching hat and gloves on. She was glad the coat hung to her ankles, but it didn't cover her feet. Her heels weren't open-toed, thank God, but otherwise her feet weren't covered by much.

She looked up at Tucker to find him watching her with a small smile.

"What?" she asked, matching his smile.

"Thinking there are more fun ways to warm up and then thinking I shouldn't be thinking that."

Kate felt the warmth rush through her and she wanted more. And not just because she felt like her nose might be freezing off.

"Cocoa, right?" she asked.

"Warm, sweet and comfortable," he agreed.

He tucked her arm in his, which should have been all of those things but was much more.

Stupid, stupid, stupid.

The simple mantra did nothing to change how she was feeling though.

They crossed the bar parking lot and followed a sidewalk that led between the city hall and another building and put them on one of the main streets around the square. She was glad he had a hold of her. Heels were not ideal for gravel parking lots or sidewalks with random patches of snow. After this, she was buying some thick fuzzy socks somewhere and not taking them off until she was back in California.

Still, walking through the crisp winter air toward the bright town square with this guy felt... not completely nice. It felt a little naughty, which was completely ridiculous. The most he'd said that was flirtatious was that he could think of better ways to warm up. That was pretty mild as far as sexual innuendos went. But pressing up against him, her body filled with a strange combination of awareness, desire and anticipation.

It was the Christmas trees. It had to be.

This side of the square, the corner south of the reindeer petting area, there was a narrow white wooden building with an open window at the front.

They approached and she could see they were selling cocoa, coffee and, sure enough, cider. The non-spiked variety though, she assumed. Of course, it wouldn't surprise her if a few people had a flask in their coat pocket and doctored their cup after it was served.

They got in line behind a few other people and Kate took her hand from Tucker's arm and put both hands in her coat pocket. That was safer.

"This is the kissing booth in the summer," he said.

She looked up at him. "What?" All she knew for sure was he'd said the word kissing.

He pointed toward the little wooden structure. Propped against the back wall was a wooden sign that said *Kissing Booth* in big red letters. The wooden sign that hung over the window now read *Hot Drinks*.

"I guess it's good they're getting year-round use out of the building," she said with a chuckle. "Though it seems kissing should be a year-round event too."

And why had she said *that*?

He chuckled and the sound was warm and rich and made her sigh. Like a big swallow of hot cocoa.

She mentally rolled her eyes. Phoebe had said there was something in the air and water in Sapphire

Falls, but Kate didn't know that it was Christmas spirit so much as it was horniness.

"But the drinks are for a good cause," he said.

There was also a sign propped up against the front of the wooden booth that said the proceeds from the drinks were going toward Christmas gifts at the nursing home.

Kate found herself incredibly touched by that. It wasn't that people where she was from weren't charitable, but here it had to be a lot more personal. Likely every single person who lived at the nursing home had family and life-long friends and neighbors here in Sapphire Falls.

"I want an extra-large then," she said with a smile.

He grinned. "Marshmallows too, I hope?"

"Of course."

"How about caramel or peppermint syrup?" he asked, reading the menu board.

She shook her head. "I think straight up and simple is the way to go."

She really wanted peppermint syrup. A lot. That sounded perfect. Peppermint hot cocoa would be very Christmassy. Perfectly Christmassy even. But maybe that was a bad idea. Maybe she was putting too much pressure on all of this being perfect. Maybe she had her expectations too high. She shouldn't have scripted it all out in her head. She shouldn't have imagined holding hands and walking through a light flurry under the stars.

She should keep things simple. Straight forward. She should look at Tucker as nothing more than a nice guy who was willing to take a total stranger to the formal.

They moved up in the line.

"Oh yeah, I love this damned town." Tucker turned to look at her.

Kate felt her eyes widen at the playful and pleased look in his eyes. "What?"

He pointed at the top of the drink station. A sprig of mistletoe hung directly above the window where people were picking up their cups.

"Oh."

Oh boy.

She'd hoped for a Christmas kiss. She'd hoped for mistletoe. She'd imagined the whole thing.

And now she was panicking.

It could never measure up. She needed to keep this simple too, like the hot cocoa.

No romantic kisses, no romantic dreams and fantasies. A nice guy, a formal, a few dances, maybe some eggnog—*not* poured all over his body—and a nice, simple, sweet Christmas in a nice, simple, sweet small town.

"I was thinking—"

She abruptly stopped thinking about anything at all the second he took her by her upper arms, pulled her up onto her tiptoes and touched his lips to hers.

It was…everything. Everything she'd imagined and then some.

Like hot cocoa with peppermint syrup.

She tasted like Christmas cookies.

That was Levi's first thought.

Not like she'd been eating them, but like she *was* a soft, sweet, delicious melt-in-his mouth cookie. And that was pretty whimsical for a guy who was used to women tasting like tequila.

Her lips should have been cold. The crisp air of the afternoon had turned downright icy as darkness fell, but her mouth was anything but. She was hot. And sweet. And he could happily spend the rest of December right here doing this.

Then she clutched the front of his coat, trying to get closer, opened her mouth and sighed.

And he amended the thought to the rest of the winter.

They didn't use tongues. It was lip to lip only. Open lip to open lip, but that softened the kiss, made it more of an exploration.

The moment he'd seen her on the bar stool, his hands had itched with the need to touch the red dress, and the curves it covered. He'd immediately imagined her long blonde hair spread out on the maroon and navy quilt in the farm's guest room. And he'd instantly started making a list of thank you gifts he could get for Phoebe and Joe.

But then she'd swiveled to look at him and everything hot and urgent and pulsing in his gut had risen to a soft, warm ball in his chest. He'd wanted to run his hand over her cheek instead of her ass. He'd wanted to make her laugh rather than scream with an orgasm. He'd wanted to know how she drank her cocoa rather than how she took her martinis.

It was the craziest fucking thing that had ever happened to him.

And he'd embraced it.

This was it. This was how it was supposed to feel when sweet, normal, happy things happened to someone. When liquor and money and sex were not part of the equation. When two people met for the first time and connected.

Maybe it was Sapphire Falls. Maybe it was the concussion. Maybe it was that he was dressed in denim. Maybe denim made people instantly normal. Or maybe it was her. Maybe this woman really did have the power to cure him of the selfish, superficial, ego-driven crap he had bottled up inside.

He cupped her cheek, simply tasting her. The kiss wasn't about arousal or a step toward sex. It was only a kiss.

And he fucking loved it.

"Ahem."

The sound of someone clearing their throat pulled them apart.

She stood staring up at him, her eyes wide, her lips pink. And he grinned. He couldn't help that—he really did love having an obvious effect on women.

But again, this was different. Rather than wanting to see her nipples get hard and her panties get wet, he wanted a faint blush on her cheeks and a sparkle in her eye.

It had to be the concussion.

But he was going to go with it.

Hear that, ghosts? I don't need any midnight hauntings. I'm good here.

"What are you having?" the guy in the window asked.

"Two hot chocolates, extra-large, with marsh-mallows," Levi told him. Those words sounded so foreign, like he was speaking another language. That also made him grin.

There were four guys inside the booth working to make drinks, taking orders and money.

Two got to work on their drinks as the one at the window said, "That'll be four fifty."

Levi handed him a hundred-dollar bill.

The guy stared at it. "Dude, I can't make change for that."

"Keep it." Levi pushed the money across the counter.

"You want to pay me a hundred dollars for two cups of cocoa," the guy clarified.

"It's a fundraiser, right?" Levi said. "That's my donation."

The guy was still looking at him strangely, but he took the money. "Well, then you can have free refills. Forever."

Levi grinned and accepted the two cups. "Deal."

He offered one to Hailey.

Hailey Conner. She was the mayor here. He wondered how people would feel about their mayor getting kissed by the stranger in the town square.

"You okay?" he asked when he realized she was staring at him.

"Stunned, actually."

He smiled and sipped. The hot chocolate was delicious. Practically perfect. But it would never beat the taste of this woman's lips. "That was a hell of a kiss."

She nodded. "And that was a lot to pay for hot chocolate."

"I have a feeling this will be the best hot chocolate of my life."

Her eyes widened at that. "Have you had a lot of hot chocolate over the years?"

And just like that it was clear they weren't talking about hot chocolate. He grinned. "Probably more than my share."

She gave a little snort like that didn't surprise her. Levi had been told before that he gave off a womanizing vibe. Whatever that meant. He didn't know any other way to be. None of the men in his family knew any other way to be. They loved women and women loved them, and Levi hadn't been raised to see that as anything other than awesome.

They walked toward the middle of the square. Around the gazebo, there were several benches and a surprising number of them were occupied. There were actually a number of people in the square. Families with kids at the gingerbread house and petting the reindeer. Couples walking hand in hand or cuddling on the benches, cups of various hot drinks in hand. Clearly, the people in Sapphire Falls were used to the brisk temperatures.

Or maybe it was that he was from Vegas and his hide was too thin for the cold air. By this time next year he'd be adjusted, he thought with a grin. He took in the scene before him and a deep breath of what he could only describe as Christmassy air. It was, admittedly, a cozy scene, and Levi was suddenly a fan of colder weather. What a great reason to get a pretty girl in his arms.

The square was brightly lit. The four huge trees were completely decked out from tip to trunk in lights and ornaments—some of which also lit up. The street lamp posts were all twisted with tinsel that sparkled and reflected the lights. Then there were the giant lighted candy canes, plastic oversized ornaments, and the gingerbread house that had lights around the eaves like any good home in a Christmassy small town.

"Want to sit?" he asked, indicating a bench that faced one of the trees. She'd wanted a tree, he'd brought her to the middle of four gigantic ones. That was how Levi did things—big, bright and better.

He frowned. He might need to squelch those urges a bit. If Phoebe was any indication of the women in Sapphire Falls, they weren't impressed with overspending and big flashy gestures. Phoebe was down to earth. It stood to reason that a friend of hers would be the same.

They sat on the wooden bench and Levi stretched his arm along the back behind Hailey's shoulders. She cuddled up against his side and he felt the heart he'd recently rediscovered expand.

This was nice.

This was the freaking epitome of nice.

He could get used to this.

They could sit here in the spring and look at the tulips coming up around the gazebo. They could come in the summer and watch the Ferris wheel turn. He knew there was a Ferris wheel from Joe's photos of the summer festival that went on each June. Hell, they could ride the Ferris wheel. Levi tried to remember the last time he'd been on a carnival ride and came up blank. Had he never ridden a Ferris wheel? Was that possible?

"I should text Phoebe and let her know that we found each other."

"Great. I'll tell Joe too." His brother was no doubt wondering how things were going.

Met Hailey. I OWE YOU. Levi grinned as he hit send. That would make Joe curious, and Levi meant it.

She sent her text and then slid closer, cupping her cocoa in both hands. Levi was hit by a combination of scents, including the chocolate from her cup, the scent of evergreen that he wouldn't be surprised to find that they piped into the square somehow to help with the whole festive feel, and the scent of vanilla that he could have sworn came from her hair.

This was really, really...*nice.*

"So you must love Christmas," he said. That was dumb. She was the mayor of a town that would put the North Pole to shame.

"Not really." She was holding her cup close to her lips as if the steam from the tiny hole in the lid would warm her.

"No?" He was surprised. "Why not?"

She looked up at him. Underneath the red knit cap she looked young and suddenly a little sad.

Did he know her well enough to tell when she was sad?

"My mom lost her mom and dad in a bad car accident on Christmas Eve when she was seventeen. Ever since then, she hasn't been able to celebrate Christmas without going into a deep depression. My dad wanted to protect her from that, so they always jet off to Hawaii and avoid the holidays completely."

"They have Christmas in Hawaii," he said, hoping that wasn't insensitive. Admittedly, his radar for sensitive and appropriate was a bit rusty. If it had ever worked.

"They do, but it's easy to avoid if you have a huge house on a private beach on Lanai."

Levi processed that. Not just the tragic story, but the fact that this woman hadn't had a Christmas growing up, that she clearly came from money with the talk of huge houses on private beaches on one of the most secluded of the Hawaiian islands, and that she'd told him all of this.

"So no Christmas trees, no Santa, nothing?" he asked.

His childhood had been unconventional in almost every way, but they'd put milk and cookies out for the big guy and they had presents under the tree every year.

"Nothing," she said. "When I got older, I started trying to do things myself. Stockings and

Christmas parties and stuff but...Christmas has kind of fallen apart on me over the last few years."

Levi found himself pulling her closer and wanting to wrap his other arm around her too.

He wanted to hug her? Just hug her? Phoebe was the only woman he hugged and, in all honesty, *she* hugged *him*. Kaelyn hugged him, but that was definitely not the same thing. She either grabbed him around one knee or she wrapped her little arms around his neck and squeezed as hard as she could. He and Joe did that bro-hug thing that guys did that was not quite a hug but was more than a handshake.

That would make this woman, the built blonde in the red dress, the first woman he wasn't related to but wanted to hug...ever.

Interesting.

"Well, this Christmas is going to be amazing," he told her.

She smiled up at him. "Yeah?"

"Absolutely."

"You're into Christmas?"

He definitely was now. "I grew up with trees and stockings and stuff," he said. "And my parents always threw a big Christmas Eve party." He didn't need to tell her that he'd walked in on his dad screwing his secretary on his desk in the den. Twice.

Or that his mother typically got drunk and had smashed at least a few Christmas plates, lit the formal dining room's curtain on fire with some ornate candelabra, twisted an ankle, cut a finger, thrown out her back and ended up in the ER. Those were the only ways to get his father's attention away from the secretary on his desk.

Which his mom didn't typically care about really, but it seemed her husband's infidelities got to her at the holidays.

Maybe deep down everyone wanted to have a nice Christmas.

Levi frowned. There was no way he could have turned out normal. Not that this was a brand new revelation, but sitting in the quaint, albeit overdone Christmas wonderland that was Sapphire Falls' town square with a woman who smelled like vanilla, Levi wished like hell he knew *a little* more about normal.

"Thank you for agreeing to do this," she said, softly.

She was looking into his eyes like she had been at the bar and he was hit by the punch of desire he'd felt then too.

What was he agreeing to do again? There wasn't anything he wouldn't agree to for this woman, but he couldn't recall the details at the moment. "The formal?" he asked finally.

She nodded. "I know it seems silly, but I'm starving for a nice, normal, traditional Christmas."

The word *starving* made him think of things *he* was feeling hungry for come to think of it.

"I completely understand," he managed while he was really wondering what would happen if he grabbed her chin and kissed her again. This time minus the mistletoe and with tongue. And with less than sweet, gentlemanly intentions.

"And, um…" Her gaze flickered away from him for a moment and she seemed hesitant.

"Anything." He meant it. His tone might have been rougher than it needed to be, but he suddenly wanted to be the one making everything just right for her.

She met his gaze again. "Would you want to spend some time together tomorrow? We could—"

"Yes."

Again, firmer than needed, but he did like the way her eyes went round and her mouth curled.

"You don't know what I was going to suggest."

"Doesn't matter. I'm in."

Her expression shifted quickly from surprised to amused to sly. "What if I want to tie you up in tinsel and keep you at my mercy until New Year's?"

Three

There was a thud somewhere in the vicinity of Levi's heart. A thud that rocked through his whole body. Just as quickly as he went from warm to burning up, it was clear that she'd realized what she'd said out loud to a near stranger.

She started to pull back, but he put his hand between her shoulder blades and brought her in. "Fucking love tinsel," he said against her lips and then took her into a kiss that definitely heated things up.

She didn't hesitate, which further fired his blood. In fact, when he parted his lips and stroked his tongue into her mouth, she moaned.

Tinsel and anything else she wanted. That was the only thing he could really think as she pivoted to lean closer. But they were sitting on a bench, and that meant she had to fold a leg up between them. Neither of them really wanted anything between them at all, so when she made a frustrated little sound, Levi took hold of her hips and picked her up to put her in his lap. Their cups of hot chocolate tipped over into the snow, but they barely noticed.

Thanks to the tight skirt on her dress, she had to sit sideways—pulling the dress up any farther would have put her at risk for frost bite in some very unpleasant places—but they were definitely closer now. And warmer.

She gripped the front of his coat in her hands like she had before. Levi kept his hands on her hips, loving the sweet weight of her against the suddenly noticeable fly of his jeans.

She tipped her head one way, he tipped the other, deepening the kiss, the tongue stroking getting bolder and faster.

She moved her fingers to the buttons on the front of his coat and as the first released, Levi caught her hands. "It's too cold here for this." Not to mention public. In a nice small town where everyone knew his brother. He really didn't have any problems with public displays of many kinds—including some with far more skin showing than he and Hailey were—but his behavior reflected on Joe and Phoebe.

And he was a little afraid of his petite, redheaded sister-in-law.

He planned to stay in Sapphire Falls for several months, hopefully the whole year, to really soak it in and let it change him. He couldn't afford to be on her bad side.

Hailey sat staring at him, pressing her lips together, looked bewildered and turned on.

He could work with both of those things.

"Let's go somewhere warmer."

He started to shift to get up, but she didn't move. Since she was on top of him, that meant he didn't get far. She was light. He could have easily picked her up and carried her off to his—Joe's— truck. But he sensed her hesitation.

Considering they'd just met, that made some sense.

Joe and Phoebe had set them up. They had no reason to fear that the other was a serial killer or anything, but that didn't mean they should hop into bed together.

Did it?

Levi pondered that for a moment. Why not? Joe wouldn't set him up with someone crazy. And Lord knew, they had the chemistry for it. He was turning over a new leaf, but he wasn't becoming a priest. Having sex with a nice girl who might expect him to show up at her grandmother's for Sunday dinner and take her to the movies on Friday night would definitely be different.

Different was what he needed.

"I have one question," she said. "Before we go to your place."

Yes.

"Whatever you want," he told her sincerely. "And if it involves tinsel, all the better." At her little grin, he leaned in and said softly, "But turnabout is fair play. Remember that."

"What if you never want to see another piece of tinsel again in your life?" she asked.

He gave her what Phoebe had labeled his bad-boy grin. "There's always candy canes if I can't take the tinsel."

She seemed to be considering that. Carefully. And thoroughly. Much to his delight.

"I may never be able to look at a candy cane the same way again. And that's just based on my imagination."

He stared. Completely surprised and as turned on as he'd ever been talking about candy. "I'm buying every candy cane in this town."

She laughed. "You can't. Other people deserve candy canes too."

Was there any chance, any chance at all, that this woman was thinking the things he was thinking about candy canes?

"Fine, we'll leave three or four. But I'm a huge fan of peppermint flavored...things."

She laughed, but it sounded breathless. "I can't believe I'm talking like this with you."

He ran a hand over the curve of her hip to her butt. "Because we just met?"

"Because you're a nice guy who's doing Phoebe a favor by taking me to the formal."

No way had Phoebe told her that. If anything, Phoebe would look at this as a favor on Hailey's part—going out with her brother-in-law, keeping him out of trouble.

"I'll tell you a secret." He ran his hand over the delectable curve in his palm. "No guy is so nice that he isn't willing to do dirty things with candy."

"Is that right?" Her grin was huge.

"Trust me."

"Any candy?"

"Any candy."

"I did not know this." She was clearly amused.

"Well, I'll tell you another secret."

She leaned in. "Can't wait."

"Women are pretty much our candy."

She pulled back a bit, licked her lips and said, "Now *that* I knew."

"Want to go make out in my truck?"

"I do. I really, really do."

Joe flopped onto his back, his breathing ragged. "Wow."

"Ditto," Phoebe agreed beside him. "You know, I love our daughter but…"

"You'll love her even more when she sleeps through the night and *not* between us in bed?" Joe asked with a grin.

Phoebe nodded solemnly. "Seriously."

"Sex on the dryer in the laundry room was really good the other day," Joe said.

"It was." Phoebe rolled to face him. "But there's nothing like fully naked, rock-the-bed sex."

Joe laughed. "I expect we'll be able to have fully naked, rock-the-bed sex again by the time Kae is, what? Fourteen and going out with her own friends?"

Now Phoebe always kept her pajama top on and one leg in her pajama pants so she could be dressed in two seconds if Kaelyn woke up and cried for her.

Joe felt himself starting to drift off to sleep. He reached over and pulled Phoebe up against his side and opened one eye to look at the clock.

Loud, completely naked sex and asleep by eleven—ten Sapphire Falls time—*yes*.

His phone buzzed on the bedside table as he felt Phoebe sigh her almost-asleep sigh.

He wanted to ignore it. Almost as much as he wanted ten straight hours of sleep. It was just a text.

But he was a dad now. He had to answer. Anything big and important would have garnered a phone call, he knew, but he wouldn't be able to fall asleep wondering about the text anyway.

He groped around on the bedside table without fully opening his eyes. But a moment later, Phoebe's phone chimed with her text message alert and he was suddenly wide awake.

He sat up in bed. "Who's texting you?" he asked, grabbing his phone. He sighed in relief when he saw it was Levi.

"Kate."

Ah, her friend from California. "Everything okay with her?" He liked Kate. She was funny and down to earth. He also loved listening to her talk to congressmen about environmental impact and climate change. He always learned something and he loved to watch the politicians underestimate her because she was a beautiful blonde. She was articulate and could put the politicians in their place almost as fast as Joe's boss, Lauren. And Kate was sweeter about it.

"Yeah, she and Tucker found each other and are having a *great* time." Phoebe emphasized great while she held her phone up for Joe to see.

"Tucker is wonderful. Having a GREAT time."

"I got all caps from Levi too," he said with a chuckle.

"Met Hailey. I OWE YOU."

He turned his phone to show Phoebe.

Phoebe read his screen and frowned. "Hailey who?"

"Hailey Conner."

Phoebe's gaze flew to his. "My Hailey Conner?"

"The only Hailey Conner either of us knows."

"Levi and Hailey met up somewhere?"

"Yes." Joe frowned at her. "At the Come Again."

"The Come Again in Sapphire Falls?"

Joe put his phone down. "What are you talking about? You knew this."

"No, I didn't."

Then something occurred to Joe. "Kate is out with Tucker?"

"Yes."

"Tucker Bennett?"

"Yes. In Sapphire Falls at the Come Again."

"Did I know about that?"

"Yes." Then Phoebe bit her bottom lip and shook her head. "I don't know. Did you?"

"I don't think so."

They'd been so crazy getting Kaelyn packed and over to grandma's house and then packing themselves and getting to the airport that it was possible that they thought they'd mentioned these things and hadn't actually gotten around to it.

"So Kate and Tucker?" Joe asked.

Phoebe nodded. "Levi and Hailey?"

"Yeah. Levi's in town for Christmas. Hailey agreed to be his date for the formal."

"Your idea?"

Joe nodded. "Levi's decided to try some new things—like not smashing his skull in or ending up dead."

"Good things to try," Phoebe said dryly. She loved Joe's brother, and his accident had shaken her. For a long time, they'd both seen Levi going down a bad path fast. They hoped the accident would be a wakeup call.

"He's convinced Sapphire Falls can be good for him like it was me. And he wanted to date a local girl. Like you."

Phoebe grinned at that. "But you set him up with Hailey?"

"She's a local girl."

Phoebe laughed. "And that's the extent of the things Hailey and I have in common."

It was true that they seemed different. Phoebe was everyone's friend, Hailey liked to boss people around and didn't really care what anyone thought of her. Phoebe's look was more natural and girl-next-door with her red curls and blue jeans, while Hailey always looked like she'd stepped out of a fashion magazine with her sleek blonde hair and designer labels.

But the women both loved Sapphire Falls and wanted the best for their hometown. They'd slowly become friends over the past few years—something that surprised them as much as anyone.

"Well, Hailey won't let Levi's charming bullshit sway her away from keeping him out of trouble," Joe said.

"Ah, you gave her a mission."

"I did." And he was counting on the mayor to accomplish all objectives—no jail time, no hang-overs, no banged-up fenders or women falling in love with Levi between now and the Christmas formal.

It was only a few days. Surely Levi could stay out of trouble that long. With help.

"So what's up with Kate and Tucker?" Joe asked.

Phoebe lifted a shoulder. "Kate wanted a wonderful Christmas for a change. No one does Christmas better than Sapphire Falls, and when I was thinking of nice country boys to take her out, Tucker came to mind."

"He'll be nice to her," Joe agreed. "I'm glad they're having fun."

Then he thought of something. "Where's she staying?"

"In our guest…" Phoebe trailed off as she realized what Joe had just realized.

Kate and Levi were both staying at their place in their guest room.

"Uh oh," Phoebe said.

"Yeah. Well, maybe Kate will stay with Tucker," Joe suggested. There was no way Levi was talking his way into Hailey's bed. Hailey was hit on almost constantly. If she wanted casual flings, she could have them all the time. But she didn't. Hailey was probably the one woman Joe knew that Levi wouldn't be able to impress. That was exactly why he'd chosen her.

Phoebe frowned. "Hey, they're having a good time. That doesn't mean they'll sleep together. Kate's a nice girl and she wants a simple Christmas."

"Nice girls have sex too," Joe said, giving Phoebe a grin. She was a nice girl and he'd gotten her out of her panties pretty easily.

She swatted him on the arm. But she seemed to be pondering something.

"What are you thinking?" he finally asked.

"I set her up with Tucker."

"Right."

"That might mean Kate stays at Tucker's," Phoebe admitted.

"Kate might go for a fun Christmas fling? Nothing wrong with that."

"No, I don't know that she would, but…it's Tucker."

"What's the mean?" Joe knew exactly what that meant.

According to all women in Sapphire Falls and the surrounding four counties, or more, the Bennett boys were everything any woman would ever want. Even the women who were happily married to city boys who knew next to nothing about corn and cows. Only three of the Bennetts lived in Sapphire Falls. The youngest, Ty, was off being a professional triathlete—whatever that actually meant—in Colorado. And now that Travis Bennett was taken, that left only Tucker and TJ as the epitome of all things manly and sexy. And TJ was a grumpy guy who liked to keep to himself.

Which was all a long way of saying that Tucker Bennett got a lot of female attention.

"It's *Tucker*," Phoebe said again, as if emphasizing his name was all the explanation needed.

And it was.

"You realize I'm your husband right? The man you love and want more than any other? The one who has made you blissfully happy?"

Phoebe smiled and patted his cheek. "Of course you are."

Joe narrowed his eyes and started to grab for her. Not because he was actually worried about Tucker, or any other guy, but because it was so fun making her say *his* name over and over again in that breathless, pleading way she did when he—

Phoebe's phone rang.

Then his rang.

Damn.

They reached for their phones at the same time.

"Hailey," he said, reading his display.

"Tucker," Phoebe said with a frown.

"Hello?" they asked simultaneously.

"Joe, put me on speaker," Hailey said.

What had Levi done? Joe pressed the button for the speaker phone. "Okay."

"Tucker is here with me."

Phoebe pushed her speaker button too and laid her phone on the comforter beside Joe's. "What's going on?"

"Well, about this gorgeous blonde in the red dress," Tucker started.

"Kate said she's having a great time," Phoebe broke in quickly.

"Oh, that's pretty obvious. To the whole town," Tucker said.

"What do you mean?" Phoebe asked him.

"I'm standing here on the steps to city hall watching her have a good time."

Phoebe frowned. "What do you mean? Shouldn't you be *with* her?"

"Yeah, well, I'm not sure her date would appreciate that," Tucker said, his tone dry.

"Her date?" Phoebe repeated. "*You're* her date."

"Uh, no, I believe that would be Levi," Hailey said. "And from the way she's kissing him right now, they're getting along great."

Kate and Levi were *kissing*?

Joe and Phoebe met each other's gaze, their eyes wide.

"They're *kissing*?" Phoebe asked.

"Yes. And Kate looks almost as good in her red dress as I do in mine," Hailey said.

So Levi had met the wrong gorgeous blonde in a red dress.

"This is okay."

"This is horrible."

Joe and Phoebe spoke at the same time.

They frowned at each other.

"Okay?" Phoebe asked.

"Horrible?"

"Yes, horrible," Phoebe told him.

"Why? Kate's a nice girl, but she's more like the girls he normally dates." She was from the city, she had money, she knew about good wine and tipping doormen and things like that. "Except she's…nice," he finished.

"Well, Levi will be terrible for Kate," Phoebe said. "Because he's like the guys *she* normally dates."

"Except that he's…" Joe prompted.

"Worse."

"Worse?" Joe asked. "How?" But Joe kind of knew what she meant.

"His relationships are all about *him*. He collects women like…" Phoebe sighed. "Like you used to."

Joe couldn't argue with that. But it wasn't like the women had really ever complained. "And I turned out well because a nice girl from Sapphire Falls finally got a hold of me," he said. "This could be exactly what Levi needs."

"Kate isn't from Sapphire Falls."

Oh…yeah.

"And she wanted a sweet, traditional, romantic Christmas with a nice guy. That's why I picked Tucker," Phoebe said.

"Thanks, Phoeb," Tucker said. "I even showed up with flowers."

"And they really are gorgeous," Hailey said. "Deep-crimson roses with white baby's breath and evergreen branches."

Phoebe smiled. "See? That's so nice. And Tucker will buy her hot chocolate in the town square and they'll drive around and look at Christmas-light displays. They can decorate his tree and make cookies and maybe ice skate and then go to the formal. Simple, nice stuff."

"Levi could take her to look at Christmas light displays," Joe protested.

"Sure," Phoebe agreed. "In *Paris*. Right after he whisks her off on his private jet to have hot cocoa in Belgium or something."

Unfortunately, Joe couldn't deny that those things were *possible*. It was more *his* style—or had been—to overdo the dramatic gestures to impress women, but Levi wasn't above throwing money around to romance a woman.

"Wow, what a jerk," Hailey muttered sarcastically.

"So you guys need to go tell them who you are," Phoebe said to the phones. "Obviously things got mixed up. I told her dark hair, blue eyes and great smile."

"Thanks again," Tucker said.

"Levi's got all of that," Hailey pointed out. "And Kate's blonde."

"And gorgeous," Tucker added. "And if she wasn't on Levi's lap right now in the middle of the square, I might go over and insist we go on *our* date."

"She's on his *lap*?" Phoebe said. She looked at the clock. "Already?"

"Spencer charm," Joe said with a grin. "You know it's irresistible."

Phoebe looked grim as she said, "That's what I'm worried about."

"Hey."

Phoebe focused on him. "She can't get her heart broken this Christmas, Joe. She's had three bad ones in a row. This was supposed to be different. Better. Special."

"It will be fine," Joe insisted. He *really* hoped that was true.

"And meanwhile," Tucker said. "I'm now without a date to the formal. What do you think, Hails? You and me?"

"No." Hailey didn't even hesitate.

"Why not?" Tucker sounded amused.

"I don't date guys from Sapphire Falls. And don't call me Hails."

"Ty calls you Hails," Tucker pointed out.

"That's...different," Hailey said tightly.

"Uh, huh," Tucker said. "Why don't I buy you a hot chocolate and you tell me all about that."

"Yes to the hot chocolate, no to the spilling my guts."

"So there *is* something to spill," Tucker said.

There was something going on with Hailey and Tyler Bennett. Everyone suspected it, speculated about it, but no one seemed to know anything for sure.

"Hailey—" Phoebe started.

But Joe grabbed both phones, shaking his head. "Gotta go guys."

He disconnected both phones and looked at his wife. There was no time to get into anything with Hailey right now. Hailey Conner could talk about herself for hours.

And Joe didn't want to hear it. He worked with politicians for a living—he had enough drama in his life.

Phoebe was chewing on her bottom lip.

"Should we call or text Levi and Kate?" she asked. "Make sure they're okay?"

"She's on his lap, kissing in the square," Joe said, setting the phones both on his bedside table, out of Phoebe's reach. "They're more than okay."

"Yeah, and they have to have figured out who they are by now right?" Phoebe asked.

"There is no way they still think they are with Tucker and Hailey," Joe said, certain about at least that one thing.

Phoebe nodded and let him pull her down and flip the comforter over both of them. She was quiet for several seconds, but Joe knew she wasn't completely done meddling.

As he reached to turn the light off, she finally spoke. "I'll call Adrianne in the morning to go over and check on them."

Four

Hailey slid from Levi's lap and he took her hand, making himself walk at a reasonable speed for high heels. Which was tough considering he wanted to run. Of course, he could throw her over his shoulder and still get a pretty good jog going.

"By the way," she said as they passed the hot chocolate stand and crossed the street on their way back to the bar.

"Yeah?"

"This is already the best Christmas I've ever had."

There was another thud near his heart. The poor thing hadn't been used in so long every hard beat was a little painful. But it was a good pain. Like stretching a tight muscle before a hard workout.

Because he wanted to give it a hard workout with this woman.

And not only in the pounding-hard-during-hot-sex way. In the way that might stretch his heart muscle further than it had ever gone before.

Levi gave her what he hoped was a casual smile. No sense in scaring her off with a wanna-fall-in-love-this-weekend? He'd told Joe he was considering staying for a year. Nothing so far had made him want to shorten that time frame.

"You know, a smart man would be grateful that it would be almost impossible to make this Christmas *worse* than your others," he said. "But no one ever accused me of being particularly bright." He stopped next to his brother's truck and turned to face her. "I don't want this to be the best you've had so far. Hell, all I have to do is put up a tree and make you cinnamon rolls on Christmas morning to do that."

She gasped softly. "Your mom made cinnamon rolls on Christmas morning?"

Well, their cook had. He took her hands. "I want to do even more than that. I want this to be everything you ever wanted Christmas to be."

And he meant it. Maybe there was hope for him yet. So far the cheesy Christmas sentiments were rolling out of him.

Take that, Christmas ghosts.

"You said you don't have a tree yet. Will you let me help with it?" she asked. The lighter, excited tone in her voice made a different type of desire shoot through him. The desire to make her happy.

Oh yeah, there was hope. Levi Spencer was going to make someone else happy, dammit. A guy who wanted to do that couldn't have a cold, black soul.

It was dark gray at worst.

"Definitely," he told her.

"And can we bake cookies?"

"Of course."

"Tonight?"

He opened his mouth to give another enthusiastic affirmation but then realized what she'd said. "Tonight?"

He'd kind of hoped to take the quilt in the guest room for a spin tonight.

She nodded, grinning up at him in a way that made him want to buy her a puppy or something while at the same time made him want to run his hand up under her skirt.

Damn, that was weird.

Sweet and sexy at the same time? Happy and horny together?

That *had* to be the concussion.

"It's almost ten at night," he said.

"Is there a bad time for Christmas cookies?" she asked.

He opened his mouth again but could say nothing other than, "No, there's not." Because that was the God's honest truth.

Besides, watching her bake was in no way going to diminish his desire for her. He'd always been easily influenced by food. He'd had a huge crush on their cook from age six to age fourteen when she'd left them. He could barely remember what she looked like, but he could still taste her macaroni and cheese.

The women he dated had no idea how to cook or bake, nor would any of them go within a hundred yards of a cookie.

Ten minutes later, they pulled up in front of Joe and Phoebe's. Joe's F150 pickup definitely made the roads and that driveway easier to navigate. Levi had put his rental car in the garage to keep any snow flurries or sleet off of it and resigned himself to driving the truck at least until Joe and Phoebe got back.

Hailey looked from the house to him and back. "I thought we were going to make out in the truck?"

He was going to get sugar in the truck *and* in the kitchen?

Oh, yeah, best Christmas ever for sure.

Kate had been disappointed when Tucker pulled up in front of Phoebe's. She wasn't ready to go in and end the night already. But things were definitely looking up when he reached over, grabbed her wrist and pulled her into his lap.

She didn't know why, but there was something about the truck that made her feel like getting dirty. Not actually dirty, but *dirty* with a guy who got dirty for a living. She knew Tucker was a farmer, and that meant he knew a lot of stuff she had hardly a clue about.

The men she dated drove sports cars and stayed in shape by going to the gym and called other people to fix things that broke.

Tucker was a guy's guy. He drove a truck that he actually used for work. His hands got dirty. He used his muscles to lift things and carry things and throw things. Of course, she wasn't completely clear on what those *things* were, but she imagined there were hay bales and buckets and barrels of…stuff. Stuff that she was also fuzzy on. Oh, and tools. She was sure he had tools and things and that he fixed stuff. Engines and tires and…other stuff.

Okay, so most of her knowledge about life on the farm was from television and movies. She was an environmental engineer and a number of her colleagues worked in soil and water in the Midwest, but her specialty was climate change and the oceans. She'd never been to Nebraska before this trip.

The bottom line was, Tucker could use his hands in ways other men she knew could not, and she was very interested in him using those hands on her.

Sitting on his lap again was nice. Even with the multiple layers of clothing between them. Which she hadn't really thought about. She was not willing to take too many off. She was still cold from sitting in the square and wasn't sure she'd ever have feeling back in her toes. She wouldn't have traded it though. The time sitting in the square had felt… magical. That was a fanciful word to use. Heck, it was a fanciful thing to *feel*. But it fit and, dammit, she was really going for magical and fanciful here. She didn't mind that everything about Sapphire Falls, from Phoebe and Joe's quaint old farm house to the hot chocolate stand in the town square, had felt otherworldly. That was what she was going for here. An escape. A vacation. Something to keep her daydreaming for the rest of the winter. Or more.

Tucker leaned into her, reaching to crank the heat.

"Don't want anything freezing off."

She laughed softly. "Very thoughtful."

"Oh, I'm talking about *my* things freezing off. I intend to keep *your* things very warm."

It seemed all he needed to do was talk and her core body temperature went up. She pulled off her cap. "I'm glad it's dark so you can't see my hair messed up."

"Another secret about men—" he said, running a hand over her hair from the crown of her head to the ends that hit her just above the curve of her lower back, "—we like a woman's hair messed up."

"Is that right?" She pulled off her gloves and unwound the scarf from her neck, suddenly thinking she could actually overheat.

"Well, I do anyway," he said. "If a woman leaves at the end of the night with her hair too perfect, I did something wrong."

Even her feet started defrosting, something she hadn't thought would happen until March.

"But my hair's messed up from the hat."

"Yeah. For now."

Oh boy. That sounded good. She wanted that. Whatever it was. Whatever he meant. Whatever he wanted.

And maybe they should define making out. Maybe country boys made out differently than city boys. Or girls for that matter.

The way she was currently feeling, she was thinking the queen-sized four poster in the guest room was about right. She just needed to keep enough of her wits together to remember to take the quilt off. That thing was gorgeous and clearly handmade. She couldn't have hot, sweaty country sex on top of it.

But then thinking became pretty secondary.

"Take your coat off. Let me get my hands on you," he said gruffly.

A thrill shot through her. She'd imagined that small town guys were gentlemen who would take their time. There would be flirting and flowers and dates where they held hands and saw movies and kissed only if there was mistletoe involved.

Part of her had wanted that.

But now, in the truck with Tucker after hot chocolate and a kiss that had nothing to do with mistletoe, she wanted fast. Not just the sex—though she was a fan of hard and fast frankly—but the whole thing. She was being swept up in Sapphire Falls, in Christmas, in these things that she'd always thought were manufactured by the greeting-card companies but was delighted to find out actually existed somewhere.

She was giving in to all of it, floating on this cloud of Christmas as it should be. December twenty-sixth would come soon enough.

She wanted to be swept up in an affair where she felt an immediate connection with a guy and fall into bed with him the first night because what they were feeling was real and strong even within only a few hours of knowing one another.

She knew that wasn't true. She knew that love at first sight wasn't real. She knew that many a girl's heart had been broken mistaking chemistry for true love. But she was going to go with it for a few days. Kind of like believing that Santa was going to find her in Hawaii every year even without a tree or chimney or cookies or a letter. In spite of her mother. Every December, her brain had tried to tell her it didn't make sense, that it had never happened before so why now. But her heart had wanted to believe so badly she'd talked herself into it.

For a few days, she was going to let herself bask in the fantasy of true love found under a piece of mistletoe.

And the best sex of her life in the front of a pickup truck.

She unbuttoned the coat and started to shrug out of it, but Tucker helped sweep it from her without her even having to wiggle much.

"Want to feel you up against me." He met her gaze as their chests rubbed against one another as he divested himself of his coat as well.

She was totally on board with that.

He tossed his coat into the seat next to them and then slid to the middle of the truck seat, taking them out from behind the steering wheel.

"The air warm enough?" he asked.

Was the air in the truck warm enough? Did Rudolph's nose light up? She nodded. "I'm very warm."

He grinned and put his hands on either of her hips and started bunching the material of her skirt higher and higher on her thighs. "You tell me if you need any more heat anywhere."

"Will do." She squirmed to help the process, and as soon as the tight skirt was high enough that she could get her knees apart—and it had to go pretty high for that to happen—she pivoted to straddle his lap.

The bulge behind his fly was evident, and she moaned softly as he pressed her against it, lifting his hips slightly to meet her. Heat was not going to be a problem.

She had to taste him, had to get her hands on as much of him as she could, had to feel him against her everywhere.

She ran her fingers into his hair, holding his head so she could kiss him deeply. But the minute his hands slid under the edge of her dress and cupped her ass—the cheeks bare because of the

89

thong she wore—she knew she was in no way in control here.

He growled softly as his hands met the bare, still-cold-to-the-touch skin. He ripped his mouth away. "A thong in December in Nebraska? Aren't you asking for trouble there?"

But it wasn't trouble from the icy temperatures that first came to mind when she looked into his eyes. "I'm not too worried about that part of my body getting real cold with you around," she told him.

He squeezed her flesh, causing tingles to shoot from his hands straight to her clit. "Damn right."

Then he kissed her again. She was holding his head, sitting on top of him, but it was clear that Tucker was taking over.

His tongue was bold and hot and stroked along hers as one of his hands boldly stroked underneath the curve of her right butt cheek. He traced the pad of his finger over the string of the thong, following it forward to where she was hot and already wet.

He pulled his mouth away again, looking straight into her eyes as he stroked over the hot silk between her legs again. "If you don't already taste like peppermint candy here, you're going to," he told her in a husky voice that made her even wetter.

She licked her lip, trying to figure out what to say other than holy shit, *yes*.

"Oh yeah, you'll get a taste too," he promised in a dark, deep voice.

Kate felt her inner muscles clench. Damn, the guy had bought her hot chocolate, cuddled her on a park bench and now was about to make her come just talking about the things he wanted to do.

Best Christmas ever.

"On second thought," she said, nearly panting. "Maybe you should buy every candy cane in town." She suddenly had some interesting holiday inspiration of her own.

"That's my girl," he whispered, covering her lips with his again.

His girl.

The only thing that phrase should have done was yank Kate out of this crazy daze and make her realize that all of this that she was feeling was impossible. It wasn't real. It couldn't be.

But instead, she climbed that much closer to an orgasm.

In a truck. With a farmer's work-roughened, tough, can-do-anything hand stroking over her.

He ran his finger over her clit. There was still a scrap of satin between them, but she felt it as if he'd touched her with a live wire. The jolt went through her, curling her toes, and she tipped her head back. She wasn't sure why she—or any woman—actually did that, but it felt good.

"Nipples," he rasped, stroking her again. "I need to taste you."

Without anything close to a rational thought, she reached behind for the zipper. So far, she was a huge fan of making out in Sapphire Falls. This was more than she got from some guys she dated for weeks. Not many could make her come apart with a single finger with her still mostly dressed.

Some couldn't even do it with them both fully naked.

The bodice of the dress gaped as she drew the zipper down and pulled the front below her breasts. She wore a bra, but it wasn't much more substantial than the thong. The cups were mere wisps of lace really.

"Damn, need more light," he said.

But that didn't stop him from leaning in and taking one of her nipples into his mouth right through the lace. He dipped his finger under the edge of her thong and stroked along her hot, wet center, circling her clit and then sliding inside of her.

She gripped his shoulders as she gasped. "*Yes.*"

He bit her nipple gently and then pulled back. "Move your bra."

Gladly. She pulled the cups down and he again took a tip between his lips. He licked and sucked, slowly sliding his finger in and out of her.

Kate was lost. There wasn't any skin for *her* to touch, suck or lick, but she was selfish enough not to want to stop what was happening to fix that. She pressed against his hand and fisted his hair in one hand, intent on keeping him right where he was until she came.

It had been a while, she wouldn't lie. But she had limited time with this guy. She was going to soak it all in. If he thought she was greedy and easy afterward, let him think it. She'd probably never seen him again.

That thought made something clench in her chest, but the next moment, he moved his hand, his fingers sliding out of her. She started to protest until she realized he was only moving to cup her from the front. He slid two long thick fingers into her, his thumb circled her clit, and she couldn't think of anything at all.

She dug her fingers into his hair and his shoulder as she felt the desire coiling quick and hot in her core.

"You sure you're not too cold?" he asked before he nipped at the hard tip of her breast.

"I'm   actually…feeling…pretty…good," she panted.

"Yeah, you are." He stroked in and out slowly again, the tight fit of his fingers dragging along her inner walls deliciously.

Sparks seemed to shoot through her and she gasped.

But he kept up with the slow, sensual pace. She tightened her muscles around his fingers. That got a deep, heartfelt groan out of him, but he kept it slow. She ground down against his hand again. That got a muttered, "Fuck". Then she spread her knees even wider. "Holy…" he breathed roughly.

But still slow. Relentless stroking, near-perfect pressure, decadent swirls over her clit. Her orgasm was building, but it was like turning the heat on the stove up by a few degrees at a time. Things would eventually boil, but it would take forever. And she was hungry *now*.

"Faster, harder," she begged. "Make me come. Please."

There was a split-second pause, then he thrust deep, pressed her clit and held his hand there. No movement, not even a tiny flick of the smallest of his finger muscles.

Her eyes flew open and she found him staring at her. The sweet, smiling guy who'd bought her hot chocolate was gone. This guy was intense. His eyes glittered in the little bit of light afforded from the yard light, the moon overhead and the dashboard lights. He looked dark and determined…and like every erotic fantasy she'd ever had.

"Say it again," he demanded softly.

"Faster," she whispered.

He shook his head once and pressed into her. "Not that."

"Harder?" It sounded like more of a question.

He dragged his thumb slowly back and forth over her clit once. "Not that."

He was in complete command of her body. It was like he held a game controller. One flick of his thumb, one press of a finger, and he controlled what happened.

She was no way restrained. The doors weren't even locked. But Kate couldn't have done anything other than what he told her to do.

"Make me come." It was a plea. Soft, breathless, husky. "Please make me come."

"Pinch your nipple," he told her.

The hand between her legs still didn't move, but she was aware of every inch of him inside of her.

She took her hand from his hair—the only true hold she'd had on him—and pinched her nipple between her thumb and finger. She gasped at the connection between the tip and her clit.

"Lean back."

She let go of his shoulder. Now she wasn't touching him at all. Of course, she was straddling his lap and she was very much against his hand, but *he* was mostly definitely touching *her*. She leaned until she felt the dash behind her. The cold plastic pressed against her shoulder blades, putting her at an incline away from him.

The shift in position changed where his fingers were pressing inside of her, and she gasped as his fingers put more direct pressure on a very nice spot. He had more room now to move his thumb over her clit.

"Keep working your nipple," he told her.

Like she'd stop. This felt amazing. She squeezed and tugged, and he *had* to feel the way that affected her where he was touching her.

He had a free hand and he used it to pull the front of her dress up farther and then the thong out of the way. It was too dark for him to see much clearly, but the idea that she was now completely uncovered with his eyes on her ratcheted her desire a notch higher. Okay, maybe three notches.

"Put your finger in my mouth."

Her eyes widened, but she took her unoccupied hand and lifted it to his mouth. He opened and she slid her finger over his lower lip to his tongue. His lips came around the digit and he sucked lightly.

"Oh my God," she gasped.

Then he started his hand moving again. He thrust in and out of her harder, faster, just as she'd asked. His thumb played with her clit. She rolled her nipple, tugged and pinched. And he sucked on her finger, moving his tongue along the length, the wet, hot, silky feel on the tip of her finger exactly what she wanted against her clit.

It was easy to imagine his mouth on her, his tongue buried where his fingers were now, and it took about two minutes for her to climb, shoot over the top and dive into the best orgasm of her life.

Her harsh breathing still filled the truck and ripples of pleasure still spiraled out from her center when he shifted his hand from under her. He lifted his hand to his mouth and tasted her.

Um…wow. No guy had ever done that. Her muscles clenched again as she watched him. Of course, no guy had ever done most—all—of the things he'd just done. To her anyway. She had a feeling he had a little experience with hands in girls' panties.

"More like sweet cookie dough than candy cane." He licked his bottom lip and gave her a wicked grin. "I'm in the mood for cookies now."

Oh, she was definitely in the mood for...*what*?

"Cookies? Now?"

"Is there a bad time for Christmas cookies?" he asked her in her own words from earlier.

"Until ten minutes ago, I would have said no. Now I want say yes. Now. Now is a bad time."

He laughed and shook his head.

He's shaking his head?

"I think this is a great time. We're gonna need the calories."

"The hot chocolate will keep me going—" she leaned in and whispered against his lips, "—for hours."

He pulled her bra and the front of her dress up and rezipped her.

She was stunned.

"You're *re*-dressing me?"

He chuckled and kissed her. "The thing is, once I get you upstairs, you're not going anywhere for the rest of tonight and probably most of tomorrow."

His words were teasing, but the tone was enough to make her very-recently satisfied girl parts say *oh goody*.

"And you want Christmas cookies," he said.

"I can wait on the cookies."

He shook his head. "The perfect Christmas is about more than sex."

She wasn't so sure about that. "What if I told you that if you don't take me upstairs right now, there will be no *candy caning* in your future?"

He gave her a very unconcerned, very sexy grin. "You'll be begging me for…caning."

She was *not* into BDSM, including—maybe especially—caning, but when he said it like that, she couldn't deny that her nipples and other parts perked up.

She could totally be into Tucker's type of caning.

She sighed. Now that her heart rate was slowing and the flashes of *more, more, more* from her clit weren't quite as intense—oh, they were still there, they'd just calmed slightly—she thought about the cookies. And more importantly, that this guy was willing to wait on sex so that she could have her Christmas cookies immediately.

That was…unexpected. And amazing. And made her want him even more.

Plus, the whole guy-baking-for-her thing? Oh, yeah, she'd be so ready to go by the time they climbed those stairs. Suddenly, she couldn't wait to see his hands buried in the cookie dough.

And there were all kind of fun things they could do with the frosting.

"Cookies it is."

He grinned. "Let's go."

Five

He was giving up sex for cookies?

The car window might have banged him even harder than the doctors thought.

But he wanted to make cookies with this woman. Not that he didn't want to do all of the other things with her. But the driving need to give her what she wanted had culminated with his fingering her to orgasm while he stayed dressed, and damned if he didn't feel completely satisfied in so many ways now anyway.

This trip was getting more and more surprising by the minute.

Plus, covering her in sugar, colored sprinkles and whatever else went into Christmas cookies seemed like a hell of a plan.

Until he could get some candy canes.

He was already hard—beyond hard—but the thought of all the things they were going to do with the candy canes made his cock press uncomfortably against his zipper.

She grabbed up her coat, scarf and hat but didn't put them back on. She stepped out of the truck onto the drive in front of Joe's house, but there was deeper snow where Levi had parked and her heels sank in. Levi rounded the truck quickly, swept her into his arms and carried her to the porch.

"Galant," she told him with a smile.

"I can't have you breaking your leg or neck walking in snow in those shoes. I've got plans for you later."

He felt a little shiver go through her and knew it wasn't from the cold. He let her down in front of the door and tipped the ceramic frog over to retrieve the key. He unlocked the door and swung it open, letting her step across the threshold before him.

She tossed the coat and other gear on the couch, kicked her shoes off and crossed to the nearest lamp as if she knew the room. Of course, she probably did. She and Phoebe were friends and she lived here in Sapphire Falls. Hell, maybe she and Phoebe hung out here a lot.

And that made him imagine them having dinner here with Phoebe and Joe. He could picture her beside him for summer barbecues, his niece's birthday parties, Sunday dinners after church.

He didn't even go to church. That was how much this woman was affecting him.

"I assume cookies happen in the kitchen," she said with a smile.

She had no idea the crazy things going through his mind, and that was probably good, Levi thought. He'd scare her off for sure. No one thought things like this after knowing each other for one evening.

He followed her through the arched doorway that connected the living room and dining room and on into the kitchen. She flipped lights on as she went.

Phoebe and Joe's kitchen was spacious with tons of cupboards and counters, a big wooden table near the window that could easily seat eight and a center island with pots, pans and various utensils hanging from an ornate metal rack overhead.

He moved to lean against one of the counters where he thought he'd have the best view. Hailey stopped by the island and turned to face him, smiling expectantly.

"So where do we start?" she asked.

"Sugar."

She looked around. Her gaze landed on four canisters of varying height next to the fridge and she pulled the one labeled *sugar* from the group. "Now what?"

He laughed. "I guess we'll need that. But I meant sugar cookies. That's what traditional

Christmas cookies are right? The ones that are in different shapes and frosted?"

She frowned. "Yes, I think so. What else do we need for those then? Flour, I'm guessing." She pulled that canister forward as well.

She was guessing? Uh, huh. She was cute. "Probably."

She gave him a funny look. "Butter? Eggs?"

"Sounds good."

She started to reach for the handle on the fridge but then dropped her hand and turned to face him. "What about paprika?"

He nodded. He knew nothing. "Sure."

She put her hands on her hips. "Paprika? Really? I may not know anything about baking, but I do know you're messing with me now."

He straightened away from the counter. "You know nothing about baking? What do you mean?"

Her eyes widened. "I mean, I don't bake."

"You don't? But you're Christmas cookie crazy?"

"Yes, I am. And the bakery down the block from my building makes amazing ones."

He frowned and stepped closer. "The bakery on the highway?"

"No, it's on a hundred-and-fifty-seventh."

He stared at her. Sapphire Falls did *not* have 157 streets, that much he did know. "What are you talking about? I figured all the Sapphire Falls girls baked."

She laughed. "They probably do."

"So *you* bake."

She shook her head. "Knowing Sapphire Falls girls does not automatically mean I know how to bake."

"I'm so confused."

"Me too. I thought *you* baked."

"Why would you think that?"

"I don't know." She shook her head. "I guess because you were all into the idea, and since *I* don't bake, I figured…" She trailed off and took a deep breath. "So the guys in Sapphire Falls don't learn to bake from their moms and grandmas?"

"I have no idea." He felt like he was missing something here.

"How do you have no idea?"

"I…" He took a deep breath and worked on refocusing. "What are we talking about?"

"That neither of us bakes."

"And that we assume most people in Sapphire Falls are comfortable in the kitchen."

She smiled at that. "Perhaps a stereotype."

"A stereotype from people who are…" And it dawned on him. "From two people who are not from Sapphire Falls."

She raised her eyebrows. "You're not from here?"

"No. You?"

"No."

"But you got elected mayor anyway."

She laughed. "Mayor? Of Sapphire Falls? Don't be ridiculous. This is the first time I've even stepped foot in this town."

Levi straightened, surprise zapping through him. "What?"

"And shouldn't you know who the mayor is?" Then she shook her head. "No, wait, you said you're not from here either."

"I'm not. My brother is."

"Who's your brother?"

"Joe."

Her eyes were completely round now. "Joe? Phoebe's Joe? Joe Spencer?"

"Yes." He was confused and exasperated. "I'm Levi Spencer. Who are *you*?"

"Kate Leggot. I'm a friend of Phoebe's. We met last year in DC."

"DC?" Levi repeated. "You're from Washington DC?" She was a city girl? Levi ran a hand over his face.

"I'm from San Francisco. I travel to DC for work a lot."

He groaned and put his other hand up to his face. She was a *city* girl. One that traveled for work. She was not a small-town girl who rarely ventured outside of her little town oasis. She was not a small-town girl who loved the simple things in life. She didn't even know how to bake.

"Dammit."

"Hey, I can hear you," she said crossly.

He dropped his hands and looked at her. This was the woman who had enchanted him from minute one. This was the woman who had made him think crazy things about home and hearth and family. Within an *hour* of meeting her.

And her name was Kate.

And she was from San Francisco.

"You do look like Joe now that I know you're his brother."

In all fairness, she looked as stunned by the revelation about their identities. "Who were you supposed to meet?"

"Tucker Bennett. He's from here. A local farmer. Dark hair, blue eyes. You?"

"Hailey Conner. Also from here. Mayor. Beautiful blonde in a red dress."

"Wow."

He studied her face. She was so beautiful. She was a city girl, presumably visiting for Christmas.

She didn't know how to make cookies and her family typically spent the holidays in Hawaii rather than in this quaint little town that he already felt getting under his skin. She wasn't a sweet, homegrown girl who could make him change his ways and save his soul. But he still wanted her with an intensity that completely shook him.

It was just like him to get into some crazy situation—accidentally, of course—that was completely opposite of what he knew he needed. It was just like him to find all of his good intentions tested and to find his willpower crumbling within the first hour. It was just like him to look at a woman, know that she was going to be trouble and decide that consequences only mattered if you were out of money and charm. And he had yet to run out of either.

But he still backed away, shaking his head. "You know what? This is obviously a big mix up. We can straighten it all out tomorrow. I'm supposed to take Hailey to the formal and you're supposed to go with Tucker. We'll go talk to them in the morning and apologize for the mistake."

Yes, that was the right thing to do. Hailey and Tucker might be upset, but they could smooth things over. One thing Levi was really good at was smoothing things over after screwing up. Practice made perfect after all.

Ha, he thought. *Christmas ghosts thought they had me, but I'm still good.*

The concussion had to be helping him here too, because this was completely out of character.

She nodded. "Yeah, okay. Maybe that's a good idea. How will we find them?"

He laughed. "I'm guessing the first person we stop on the street will know them both and exactly where to find them."

She smiled at that. "You're probably right."

"So we'll…" *God, she's beautiful.* "We'll do that then," he finished lamely.

She nodded. "Okay."

She shoved the canisters of sugar and flour back into place on the counter and started for the door. He followed.

They crossed to the staircase and each had a foot on the bottom step before they realized—

"You're staying in the guest room?" she asked.

"Uh. Yeah. I mean, I thought so."

"Phoebe and Joe must not have known the other invited someone to stay."

"I guess."

Well, this was awkward. Or awesome.

Levi swallowed hard and gripped the hand railing. No, dammit. This was not an excuse to take her on that fancy quilt. He could easily walk upstairs, get his stuff and come back down to sleep on the couch. Alone.

A whiff of vanilla hit him and he almost groaned out loud.

Okay, not *easily*.

Still, he could pass this test. He *needed* to pass this test. The universe was putting temptation and justifications and a *brain injury* in his path to see what he was made of. He had to be made of more than expensive liquor, risqué behavior and regrets.

"I'll get my stuff and crash on the couch."

She opened her mouth to reply and Levi's hand squeezed the banister. If she *asked* him into her bed, there was no hope for him to resist.

"Thanks," she said softly.

They climbed the stairs without speaking and headed for the guest room. When Levi stepped through the doorway behind her, he looked around. "How did I miss your stuff already in here?"

She crossed to the dresser and pulled a drawer open. "I don't know. My stuff is right here."

He ignored the fact that the drawer she'd opened was full of a variety of soft colors, silk and lace. Or tried to. He cleared his throat and thought about the fact that she'd unpacked. "You put your stuff in drawers when you travel?"

She pushed the drawer shut and crossed her arms over her stomach. "It helps keep the wrinkles out and makes me feel more settled."

He nodded and grabbed the bag he'd tossed onto the bed, stuffed the two shirts and a sock that were spilling out back into it and headed for the door. The sooner he was a floor away from her the better.

Maybe.

He was to the top of the stairs when she said, "Hey, Levi?"

He turned. "Yeah?"

"Tonight was…really nice."

It had been.

He could pull off nice. Good to know.

"Yes, it was."

"So…I'll see you tomorrow."

He gave her a nod. "You will."

He turned and continued down stairs before he could grab her and kiss her and toss all his good soul-saving intentions out into the snow.

He would see her tomorrow. And then she would see Tucker Bennett.

That made his newly revived heart hurt.

And he thought maybe he remembered why he'd stopped using it.

Kate was awake at six a.m. and lying awake in bed debating the wisdom of going downstairs. Ever.

Tuck—no, *Levi*—was down there. The man that she'd made a total ass of herself over the night before. She hadn't even known his real name but she'd been entertaining fantasies about how the next few days would go. And they hadn't been limited to candy canes and sex by Christmas tree light. They'd included sleigh rides and cuddling by the fire and exchanging special gifts that represented something about their time together and even staying in touch after the week was over.

She was kicking herself. The fact that this Christmas disappointment hurt even more than the past three was her own damned fault. She'd built this thing up to being something so big, so wonderful, so *perfect* that it had been doomed to fail.

Finally, the need for the bathroom and coffee urged her out of bed.

She tiptoed to the bathroom with her clothes and toiletries clutched against her chest. She showered and blow dried her hair and by the time she was dressed and on the steps, she'd decided that she was going to treat Levi exactly the way she would have if she'd known he was Joe's brother last night. She'd be polite, friendly—they had Phoebe and Joe in common after all—and they would then go to town and find Tucker. And Hailey. Just as he'd suggested.

The fact that she hated Hailey Conner and had never even met the woman didn't mean anything.

She managed to get past the couch where Levi was still asleep without stopping.

The inching she'd done through the living room still technically counted as moving.

But she was only human. He was on his back, shirtless, wearing only black silk boxers. How could the guy be warm enough? It was chillier down here than it had been upstairs, but he still had only a light fleece blanket twisted around his legs. Most of his muscular right thigh showed as did both of his big feet. His upper half was completely bare, the contours of the muscles of his chest, abs and shoulders made her eyes widen. Seriously? She'd had no idea what had been hiding under his winter coat. His dark hair was mussed and dark stubble shadowed his jaw.

He didn't even snore.

Damn.

She kept her eyes off of his boxers—pretty much—and she ignored all of the memories from his truck the night before.

Except when she looked at his hand and noted how long and thick his fingers were.

She flushed and hurried the rest of the way to the kitchen.

Caffeine.

That fixed a host of problems.

Thankfully, Phoebe and Joe had a coffee pot and plenty of grounds.

She was almost through her second cup when she heard the knock at the front door.

Someone was at the door? Huh?

She started for the living room but heard the door open before she hit the carpet. Levi had the door open and was smiling at whoever was on the other side.

"Hi, I'm Adrianne. You must be Levi."

"Hey, Adrianne. You got it."

It was a woman. And Levi was still only wearing black silk boxers.

A shot of something that could have been jealousy—if she cared that he was mostly naked in front of another woman, which she did *not*—went through her. It was probably concern. He was mostly naked and it was cold outside.

"I brought these over for you. Welcome to Sapphire Falls."

Levi reached for something and came back with a huge platter.

"Are these Christmas cookies?" he asked.

Kate felt her heart trip. Cookies. That would definitely help.

"They are," the woman said. "I own Scott's Sweets down on the highway."

"Noticed your shop on my way into town," Levi told her. "Had you on my to-do list while I'm here."

The woman's little laugh made Kate feel that same stab of jealousy—or concern. She stepped into the doorway, very much in Levi's personal space.

"Hi, I'm Kate."

"Nice to meet you, Kate, I'm Adrianne."

Adrianne looked like a nice woman. She was short and curvy and blonde. She wore blue jeans, brown leather boots and a navy-blue coat.

"Thanks for the—" Kate's attention dropped to the bright red ceramic platter with white snowflakes around the edge. The cookies were magnificent, "—*cookies*."

Levi chuckled at her reverent tone, but she couldn't help it.

Her mouth was already watering.

She lifted the edge of the plastic wrap over the top and snagged a snowman. She bit into it and groaned.

Levi cleared his throat and she looked up at him. There was heat in his eyes that took her breath for a moment and she could only stare. He lifted a hand and ran his thumb along her bottom lip. Her tongue traced the same path on her lip as he lifted his thumb to his mouth and licked the smudge of white frosting.

Holy…

"So do you both have everything you need?" Adrianne asked.

Kate jerked back, her gaze going from Levi's mouth to the other woman. Then back to Levi… and his naked chest.

"Phoebe asked me to stop by and check in," Adrianne added.

"We, um…we're…"

"Good," Levi said, his eyes on Kate. "We're really good."

Kate nodded dumbly. They were something, and it didn't feel *bad*.

"Hey, Adrianne," Levi asked. "I don't suppose you know where Tucker Bennett lives?"

He moved his gaze from Kate to Adrianne and Kate could breathe again. She took another bite of cookie. Sugar and fat never failed her. She loved them and they were true.

"I do," Adrianne said with a grin. "About three miles south of here."

"I don't suppose you know if he has his tree up yet?" Levi asked.

"Actually, I know that too. Yes, he does. He's also decorated two outside in his yard."

"And does he have any of these cookies of yours?" Levi pulled another cookie from the tray, a wreath with thick green frosting and red candy balls, and handed it to Kate.

Well, who was she to argue? She took it and bit into it.

Adrianne laughed. "No, not yet."

"I'll pay you a thousand dollars *not* to take any cookies to Tucker," Levi said.

Adrianne looked from him to Kate. Kate somehow tore her attention from him to meet Adrianne's curious, amused eyes.

"Tucker prefers my peanut-butter balls anyway," Adrianne said.

"How about you, Kate? You like peanut butter balls?" Levi asked.

"Not as much as cookies," Kate admitted around the bite of the one she'd just taken.

"Well, there you go," he told her. "You can go meet Tucker, who has already decorated his tree and has no cookies, or you can stay here with me, help me pick, cut down and decorate a tree *and* have cookies. Your choice."

Kate felt her eyes widen. She had a choice? As in, if she picked him, they would still hang out and he'd forget about Hailey? "What about your date to the formal?"

"I haven't asked her yet, but I'm hoping she's standing right here with me now."

Kate's heart tripped. *Yes, yes, yes!* But she didn't let on that he could have whatever he wanted from her.

"You're going to go cut down a tree for us?" she asked.

She noticed that he noticed the *us.*

"Yep."

"Do you…" She had to be careful here and not tromp on his male ego. Even if it was a city-boy's ego.

"Do you know how to cut a tree down?" Adrianne asked. Her grin said that she knew it might bruise his ego but that she had to ask.

"Chainsaw," Levi said.

Adrianne nodded. "Can I make a suggestion then?"

"Sure."

"There's a Christmas tree farm not too far away. Take the highway eight miles east. There will be signs."

"Got it. Perfect." Levi turned to Kate. "You coming?"

The chance to not only decorate a tree but to actually pick it out, cut it down and drag it home.

Hell, yes. But maybe she shouldn't let on how much she wanted to do this. And that it had as much to do with him as it did with the tree.

He moved in a little closer, fully facing her now, holding the plate of cookies out of the way so he could press her up against the doorframe. "Hey, Adrianne?" Levi asked, his eyes still locked on Kate's.

"Yeah?"

"Is there a place to get candy canes between here and the tree farm?"

Kate's heart tripped again, and this time felt like it flipped over.

"A few places. The grocery store, the gas station, we have some at Scott's Sweets. I think the diner even has some up by the register," Adrianne said.

"Awesome." Levi's voice was gruff and it made heat swirl through Kate's belly. "So what do you say, Katie? Wanna go get a tree with me?"

Katie. No one had ever called her Katie.

But she didn't mind.

And at least he wasn't calling her Hailey.

"Yeah, I do," she said, her own voice husky.

Adrianne laughed softly. "Poor Tucker."

For a second, Kate had forgotten she was there.

"Tell Tucker…" Levi trailed off as if not sure what exactly his message to Tucker was.

"That it's nothing personal?" Adrianne suggested.

Levi lifted a hand and traced a finger down Kate's cheek. "Oh, it's definitely personal."

"Right. Okay." Adrianne cleared her throat. "Things are clearly good here. I'm going to go." She was halfway down the porch steps when she turned back. "The tree farm thing. When do you think you might go over there?"

Levi stepped back and Kate pulled in a big breath. "An hour or so, I suppose, why?" he asked.

"Oh, good. You don't want to wait too long," Adrianne said. "It's close to Christmas. The good ones might all be gone."

"Thanks."

Adrianne gave them a wave and headed for her car. They stood in the doorway as she drove off. Then Levi turned back to Kate.

"So you're staying? With me?"

She nodded. "Yes."

"I should tell you that last night I was determined to stay away from you, to make sure you met Tucker and went to the dance with him."

"Because?"

"Because I need to prove to myself that I can be a good guy and do something for someone else. Something that doesn't benefit me at all. Maybe even something that hurts a little. And trust me, you going out with Tucker would hurt."

He lifted his hand and ran his palm down over her hair from her head to the middle of her back.

"But then I saw your face when you saw the cookies."

Yeah, she'd been more excited than a grown woman probably should be about snowman cookies. "And?"

"I wanted to make you light up like that. I want to give you all the things you're looking for this Christmas. And surely that makes me a good guy, right? Wanting to make someone else completely happy?"

She put her hand over his heart. "Why so worried that you're not a good guy?"

"Because I'm not."

"I find that hard to believe."

He gave her a wry smile. "I'll tell you about it, but not until we're out cutting down a tree and decorating. You'll be more forgiving of me then."

She studied his face. There was something there, something hopeful, and something that looked like…fear. He was afraid that he could tell her something that would make her not want to be with him?

That should probably freak her out.

But it didn't. Because he was worried about it. A true jerk, someone she couldn't trust, wouldn't care. And that was what she saw in his eyes. He cared. About what she thought and felt about him.

Besides, this was Joe's brother.

"Okay," she agreed. "Let's go."

He gave her a relieved grin and turned into the house, pulling her with him by the hand. "I'll get dressed."

"Okay." She laughed. Talk about relieved. So he wasn't the guy she was supposed to be spending this Christmas with. He was the guy she wanted to spend Christmas with.

He was dressed and at the door twenty minutes later.

Kate was through her third cup of coffee. And her sixth cookie. She quickly brushed the crumbs from her mouth and the front of her shirt while surreptitiously rearranging the cookies on the tray so it wasn't quite so obvious she'd eaten half a dozen, then she turned to face him.

"Ready?"

He looked excited. And sexy.

His hair was still wet, even blacker than when it was dry. He hadn't taken time to shave so his jaw was sexily scruffy. He was dressed in blue jeans and a blue T-shirt that made his eyes glow even brighter blue.

Damn.

"Don't forget the candy canes," she said as she made a beeline for the living room where her coat and gloves and purse were on a chair near the front door.

He grabbed her hand as she passed. He pulled her in and dipped her back, kissing her hot and sweet before setting her back on her feet and grinning. "I dreamed about candy canes last night."

"Maybe the tree can wait."

He laughed. "No way. If we're going to get to know one another, I'm going to need all the brownie points I can get."

"That bad, huh?"

"Shameful."

"Shameful? Or shameless?"

He tipped his head. "A lot of both."

"Sounds like fun stories."

"Stories that lead to a car accident, a concussion and me here in Sapphire Falls changing my life."

A car accident and concussion? She lifted a hand to his head. "Are you okay?"

"I'm getting better every second I'm with you." He took her hand and pressed a kiss to the center of her palm.

She felt tingles shoot through her body, but she still asked, "Is this the result of the concussion?"

He shrugged. "If it is, I never want to get over it."

She smiled and then frowned. "Wait, you mean this might actually all be a product of a brain injury?"

He kept hold her hand when she tried to pull away. "It's not a brain injury. It's a concussion."

"Which means your brain was tossed around like a rubber ball inside a box."

"Yeah, kind of. I'm fine though. Doc wants me to take it easy. Make some lifestyle changes."

She nodded as it hit her she knew almost nothing about this man except that he knew what he was doing with his lips and fingers. And he was Joe's brother. Which meant he'd grown up in Vegas in their family's casinos and had money on level with Trump. Her eyes went wide. "You're rich," she blurted out before she could think better of it. Then she blushed. "Sorry. I just realized I know some things about you because of what I know about Joe."

He nodded. "I'm rich. Part of my problem."

Some people might have scoffed at that, but she actually knew what he meant. His money allowed him to be less responsible in some ways. Maybe many ways.

Her family had money too, and that was what had allowed her mother to run from and self-medicate her depression rather than dealing with it. She could have afforded great therapy, but she'd chosen the path of denial and liquor and shopping. It wasn't only Christmas that had suffered from her emotional turmoil, but it was the thing that was most obvious to her children. At least until they'd gotten a lot older and realized Mom was so fun because she preferred to cover up any and all pain or difficulty with trips—to the beach, to the mall, to Disney World.

Dealing with pain and confronting difficult things was definitely harder as a grownup since Kate hadn't had a role model or any practice.

Hence Kate's plan to hibernate in her apartment and ignore Christmas completely.

It seemed that every time she'd put herself out there and tried to make some happy memories, it had blown up in her face. She'd begun to think her mom was right.

But then Levi had come along.

"It wasn't your money that helped you give me a wonderful night last night, and cutting and decorating a Christmas tree, cuddling by the fire and watching Christmas movies on Netflix won't cost a thing."

His expression changed from one of self-deprecation to something that almost seemed like affection. "You're right. The hot chocolate cost me, but everything else was all me."

He seemed so pleased by that she couldn't help but grin and slip her arms around his waist in a hug.

Levi seemed startled for a moment, as if he wasn't sure how hugging worked, but Kate held on, and a few seconds later, she felt his arms around her.

The guy was a fantastic kisser, but he wasn't a bad hugger. Not at all.

Reluctantly, she finally pulled back. "I want to hear some background to these shameless tales while we're out," she told him. "Then I promise when we get back here, it's all Christmas and joy and cheesy childish stuff. Anything we've always wanted out of Christmas and never had."

He hadn't fully released her from the hug and ran his hands down to rest on her butt. "Two things that I want aren't childish at all."

Immediately, her whole body responded. Her first instinct was to shed every single stitch she was wearing. And that was just her first instinct. She took a deep breath. "What are those?"

"I want to sit in front of the fire, wrapped up in a blanket with you and drink wine," he said, pointing to the table in front of the couch.

That sounded heavenly. "Done," she said.

"And the other involves the floor too."

"Okay."

"I want to strip you down, piece by piece, kissing everything I unwrap like you're the best gift I've ever gotten. Then I want you to ride me with only the fireplace and the tree lighting up this room."

No, *that* sounded heavenly. She stared up at him. Sex by Christmas tree light. It was like he'd read her mind.

"We'll have to wait until dark so that's the only light in here," she said.

Of course, they could practice on the bed upstairs, or on the kitchen counter, or in the shower, or on Phoebe's huge, sturdy dining room table...

"Then we'll wait. It will build the anticipation. Make it even better."

She wasn't so sure about that. There was something to be said for immediate gratification. Not to mention the fact they only had a few days together. "But maybe—"

He silenced her with a kiss. An instantly hot, bold, arch-against-him-and-moan kiss.

Nearly two minutes later, he finally raised his head. "Let's go get a tree."

Right. A tree.

Dang, her head was still a little swirly from that kiss.

But she did want a tree. And he wanted to get her a tree. And that was the nicest thing anyone had done for her in a very long time.

Except maybe Phoebe insisting she come to Sapphire Falls in the first place.

Six

"What about this one?" Levi asked.

Levi was in love. With Christmas trees, with crisp December Nebraska air, with the fact that the people at the gate had greeted them warmly and handed Kate and him each a candy cane. And then readily given him three more when he'd asked. They were tucked securely in his coat pocket and he was feeling alive.

He'd been completely sincere when he'd told Kate that he had intended to stay away from her right up until the second he'd seen her eyes light up because of a tray of cookies.

He wanted to make her light up—in so many ways.

That had to mean his soul was getting to be more of a steel-gray color than charcoal-gray.

And he was having a hell of a good time. As they'd driven to the farm and begun walking through the trees, they'd taken turns sharing family stories—good ones and bad ones. Kate's family had been no perfect white-picket-fence family either, and that made him feel more comfortable with her. He didn't actually think that just because someone lived in a small town in a cute house they were guaranteed happiness and sunshine all the time. But now that he'd thought about it more, he was a little intimidated by the idea of living in a place like this with a girl from here. Nothing was perfect, and the higher the expectations for perfection were, the bigger the disappointment when things didn't work out.

That was why he worked to keep people's expectations of him low.

He could really frustrate a girl who had been raised in Sapphire Falls. With Kate, maybe not so much.

Strange reason to like someone, but being able to be himself and not feel like a complete failure was probably kind of important for a long-term relationship.

And, yes, he'd started thinking of things with Kate in terms of long-term.

"Levi, that tree is like fourteen feet tall," Kate said with a laugh.

He lifted the chain saw, feeling manly and stupid at the same time. He'd been surprised to find the thing in Joe's garage, but he figured if Joe was using a chainsaw, then he could handle it. It couldn't be too hard. He had a degree in business and finance. Technically. He hadn't actually used his degree in… ever. But he wasn't a dumbass.

"So? I think size matters in Christmas trees." He waggled his eyebrows.

She rolled her eyes but was still grinning. "Phoebe and Joe's house does not have fourteen-foot ceilings."

Ah, good point. He lowered the chainsaw and moved a few trees farther into the row they were in.

"How about this one?" He didn't hear anything behind him so stopped and turned.

Kate was standing in front of a tree a row over. She was looking up at it like she'd never seen anything more beautiful.

Levi stayed where he was, content to watch her for a minute. She looked young and happy and vulnerable. It hit him that this was very important to her. He'd known it, he'd heard her say it, but looking at her now, as if a childhood dream had just come true, he found himself a bit choked up.

Finally, she took a deep breath and pulled her gaze from the tree. She looked around and then saw him standing there. Her lips spread into a big smile and he realized that she'd been looking for him.

He walked toward her. "Hey."

"This one," she said.

"Okay." He stepped back from her, his hand on the starter rope, but as he was about to pull he heard, "Levi! Kate!"

He lowered the saw again and turned.

A big guy and a gorgeous brunette were coming toward them with huge smiles.

"Lauren? Hi! Oh my gosh." Kate and the woman embraced.

"Hi, Adrianne told me you guys were coming out here. I had to stop by and say hi," Lauren said.

"Hi, I'm Travis Bennett," the man said, extending his hand to Levi. "You're Joe's brother, right? Joe's been working out on my farm with me for a couple of years now."

Levi recognized Lauren's name. She was one of Joe's bosses. And Levi knew Joe wasn't actually doing farm work. He was the PR and government-relations guy for Lauren's company, Innovative Agricultural Solutions. He hung out on the farms with the farmers so he knew what he was lobbying for in Washington.

"Nice to meet you," Levi shook Lauren's hand too. "Thanks for keeping my brother employed," he told her.

"It is keeping him out of trouble?" Lauren asked.

"It's keeping him from using our private plane at least. More availability for me," he told her.

She laughed. "Joe's the best. But don't tell him I said that. He's cocky enough."

"Runs in the family," Levi said smoothly.

"Oh, that and a few other things, I'm guessing," Lauren said.

Yep, she was one of those women it was hard to charm. She saw through bullshit. He could tell within two minutes of meeting her.

Which meant she was the type he usually stayed away from.

He looked at Kate. Now though, he might not have to resort to bullshit. Maybe he could just be himself.

Kate was staring at Travis. In fact, she was checking Travis out.

Oh really? Levi turned to face her, watching her with a mix of interest, amusement and, yep, jealousy. He wasn't used to feeling jealousy. It was an interesting emotion.

She looked Travis up and down...and clearly liked what she saw.

Was it the jeans that had clearly been washed a million times, or the heavy jacket or the clunky boots he wore? As far as Levi could tell, Travis Bennett fit the part of a down-home farmer perfectly.

"Bennett?" she finally said. "Are you related to Tucker?"

"He's my younger brother," Travis said with a nod.

"Do you…um…look a lot alike?"

Levi scowled.

Lauren laughed. "They're definitely related. I got the hottest one though." She slid her arm around Travis's waist and he kissed the top of her head.

"Huh," was Kate's reaction.

Levi gave her a look. She seemed to shake herself slightly and had the grace to blush.

Yeah, he'd show her all kinds of reasons to be glad she'd mistaken *him* for Tucker last night when they got back to the house.

"What are you guys doing?" Travis asked, eyeing the tree behind Kate.

They were on a Christmas tree farm a few days before Christmas and Levi was holding a chainsaw. This seemed self-explanatory. "Picking out our tree," Levi said, emphasizing *our*.

Which was stupid. Kate might like looking at Travis, but Travis was clearly *with* Lauren. Travis tucked one hand into the front pocket of his jeans and put the other on the back of Lauren's neck under her hair. She leaned into him and Levi felt the damnedest ache in his chest.

He wanted that.

It was such a foreign thought that it almost knocked him over.

"You going to cut it down?" Travis asked Levi.

Well, he was holding a *chainsaw*. "Yeah."

Travis nodded and didn't say anything more.

Was he going to stay and watch?

Dammit.

Levi didn't really know what he was doing, and beside the other man, who was obviously dressed for outdoor work and who had probably wielded a chainsaw a thousand times, Levi was acutely aware of the fact that he wore black Oxfords, his brother's jeans and a coat that cost more than Travis's pickup.

"This tree is pretty big," Travis finally said, studying the tree.

"Yeah." What the fuck else was he going to say?

"I don't think I could handle that tree on my own," Travis said.

Levi pretended to study the tree and gave what he hoped was a manly grunt.

"I mean, I'd want two saws and four hands on that thing for sure," Travis added.

"Huh." Levi pretended to be considering that. Two chainsaws and four hands? What had he gotten into here?

"I could help you out," Travis offered. "I have my chainsaw over in my truck. It's no problem."

Ah, he was a man who *traveled* with a chainsaw. Levi had been impressed that Joe even had one in his garage. If Travis ran into things he needed to chainsaw on a regular basis, then Levi might even be a little smitten with Travis—in a purely bromance kind of way.

He was comfortable with that.

He tried not to look too eager. He nodded and gave a shrug. "Sure. That'd be great."

"Why don't you ladies go over and check out the ornaments and stuff," Travis said. "We'll get this thing cut and loaded up."

There was an area that was made up of several long folding tables set up and draped with red and white tablecloths. On the tops was a huge display of locally made ornaments, photo frames, wall hangings, wreaths, yard signs and baked goods.

"Oh, but I was—" Kate started.

But Lauren wrapped an arm around her shoulders and started in the direction of the crafts. "Let me show you the candles Mrs. Pierce makes. They're amazing."

The women wound between the trees and were soon out of sight.

"Let's go." Travis clapped Levi on the shoulder and turned him in the opposite direction.

"Where are we going?" Deeper into the trees with a guy he didn't know and a chainsaw? He'd seen this horror movie.

"To get you a tree," Travis said with a chuckle.

They stepped out from the rows of live growing trees into a fenced-in area that had already-cut trees on display.

Understanding dawned. "We're getting one that's already cut."

Travis laughed. "For sure. Cutting a tree down is hard work, and the one you picked is enormous."

"You can't actually cut a tree down?" Levi asked.

"Oh, sure I *can*, but why? These guys already went to the trouble." Travis started forward, looking through the displayed trees until he found one that looked a lot like the one Kate had picked out. "Here you go."

"Kate might be disappointed if I don't actually, you know, act all manly and tough."

Travis slapped him on the back. "She'll never know. Once it's loaded in the truck, she won't be able to tell if it's the one she picked or not. Have her help you drag the thing into the house and put it up. It'll be heavy and will look a lot bigger once it's inside—she'll never know this isn't the one back there."

"You sound like you speak from experience," Levi said suspiciously.

"Damn right," Travis said. "I cut Christmas trees down with my dad every year growing up. It's cold, hard work. Last Christmas was the first one Lauren and I were together, so I cut the tree down with her watching. This year, I already had the thing in the corner of the living room when she got home from work. She figured I'd cut it down. Trust me, you won't lose man points because she'll *assume* you did it. I'm your witness." Travis looked him over and then bent and grabbed a handful of snow that also contained dirt and pine needles. He threw the mess on the front of Levi's coat.

Levi watched as the loose snow ball exploded against his chest and scattered dirt and needles over the expensive wool.

"That's better," Travis said with a nod.

Levi sighed. He was recalling some of the reasons he wasn't really an outdoorsy guy. He liked boating and skiing. He wasn't a bad surfer, liked to snorkel and could absolutely lay on a beach or a pool with the best of them. Digging, cutting and building things…not as much.

"Okay, let's load it up." Travis pulled gloves from his pocket and slipped them on, then he grabbed the trunk. "Get the branches. We'll tie it up and throw it in your truck."

Levi wished he had gloves. He grabbed the prickly branches. "It's Joe's truck," he felt compelled to say.

Travis nodded. "Yeah, I know, man."

But Levi didn't feel judged. He did, however, feel determined to learn how to turn on a chainsaw at some point in his life.

"How about this one?" Lauren asked, holding up a gorgeous, hand-painted ornament. It read *Our First Christmas*.

Kate's throat got a little scratchy and she shook her head. "I don't think so."

"You don't want to remember this Christmas?"

There was no way she was ever going to forget this Christmas. "It's just that it implies there will be other Christmases."

"You don't think there will be?" Lauren asked.

Kate definitely remembered that Lauren was a straight shooter.

"I know there won't be," she said, though her voice sounded funny. "This was only supposed to be a date for the formal anyway. And it was supposed to be with Tucker. Levi and I don't live in the same place and we'll both be going home after Christmas."

"Long distance sucks," Lauren said. "But it's not impossible. There's the phone, texting, email, Skype. Sexting. Sex-Skyping." She grinned.

"You've sex-Skyped?" Kate asked.

"Of course. Travis travels with me when he can, but it's not always possible."

Kate knew all about Lauren's company that she owned with her best friend, Mason Riley. Lauren traveled between Sapphire Falls, Chicago, DC and Haiti—where their primary growing program was flourishing in some of the poorest villages in the country—and to some of their newer program locations in Africa.

"But you guys make it work." Kate couldn't deny that her heart thumped at the thought of seeing Levi again after Christmas was over.

"We sure do," Lauren said with a grin. "Married and expecting a baby."

Kate's eyes widened and her gaze dropped to Lauren's stomach. "Really? Congratulations." The stunning brunette wasn't showing a bit and looked positively radiant.

Lauren's hand went to her lower abdomen. "Thanks. It's terrifying but wonderful."

"You moved here to Sapphire Falls from Chicago, right?" Kate asked. "And you love it here?"

"Even when I tried *not* to love it here." She laughed. "I didn't want to be stuck here, tied down."

"Why not?" Kate asked before she could stop herself. "This seems like such a great place." Part of her wanted Lauren to tell her that her impression of Sapphire Falls wasn't real, that it wasn't nearly as wonderful as it seemed. Part of her also wanted Lauren to confirm that it was, indeed, everything that it seemed to be.

Lauren's smile was full of affection. "Their coffee sucks and I have to shop online for almost everything. Heaven forbid you need an ingredient for a recipe after six p.m. I've had to teach them to make a decent appletini and you can't keep a secret—like, I don't know, being *pregnant*—for more than three seconds. You end up spending all your time with the same people over and over again and hearing the same stories over and over again and going the same places over and over again." She sighed happily. "And it's awesome."

Kate felt choked up.

It was the stupidest thing to desire, but part of her wanted to be in a place where everyone knew everything about her—and loved her anyway.

That was the key, of course. Being accepted. She was accepted with her colleagues and friends in San Francisco, but she also kept a lot of herself hidden.

She had a feeling the people in Sapphire Falls could get her to spill her secrets.

Her gaze landed on an ornament. It was a ceramic depiction of the Sapphire Falls town square, hand painted in blues and whites and silvers. The gazebo was there, the hot chocolate stand, the four big trees…everything.

"I think this is the one I want." She lifted it from the box.

Lauren nodded. "Definitely."

They paid for their purchases, including more Christmas cookies and some fudge from Scott's Sweets.

"Think the guys are done with the tree?" Kate asked. She took a bite of fudge and moaned.

Lauren laughed. "Yes, I'm sure they're done."

"Really? I have no idea how long it takes to cut a tree down."

"Yeah, well, longer than this, but they're not cutting it down."

"They're not?"

Lauren shook her head. "I'm sure Travis talked Levi into getting an already-cut one. But play along. It makes them feel manly to have us think that they did it."

Kate laughed. "You guys showed up because Phoebe and Joe called and told you they were concerned about our safety out here with a chainsaw, right?"

"Actually, Adrianne called us after she stopped by this morning and heard the plan."

Kate was amazed. "You all really do take care of each other, huh?"

Lauren linked her arm with Kate's. "Some call it meddling. We like to refer to it as semi-forced love."

Kate felt her eyes sting and had to blink rapidly. Only one thought was on her mind—they wouldn't have to even semi force the love here on her.

It took Kate and Levi far longer than it should have to haul their tree from the truck to the porch, through the front door and into the perfect corner in the living room.

Of course, it also took a while to rearrange Joe and Phoebe's living room to make that corner perfect.

Still, Kate could not deny that it was everything she'd imagined as she stepped back and took in the sight of the evergreen towering to the ceiling in the corner between the staircase and the fireplace. It would be the first thing seen when someone stepped in the front door.

She felt Levi move in behind her. When he wrapped his arms around her, she leaned into him and wished that this Christmas could last for a year. Or ten.

And to think that only a few days ago, she'd been planning to skip Christmas entirely.

She turned in his arms and went up on tiptoe to kiss him.

Levi didn't even hesitate. He tunneled his fingers into her hair, pulled her closer with a hand on her ass, and deepened the kiss.

Fire seemed to lick through her, and Kate wrapped a leg around one of his. She pulled her lips away only enough to say, "We have candy canes."

"We also have decorating and movies and cuddling to do."

She pulled back farther. "You don't want to have candy cane sex now?"

"I do. You have no idea how much."

"I don't see the problem."

"Once I get you naked, that's all I'll be able to concentrate on. Until possibly January twenty-something."

That was sweet…and frustrating as hell.

"Should I tell you how *I* plan to use my candy cane?" she asked.

He flexed the hand on her butt but shook his head. "Please don't."

"It's really good. There's licking and sucking involved."

He groaned. "Decorating, movies, cuddling. Decorating, movies, cuddling," he muttered. "Decorating, movies, cuddling."

She laughed. "Repeating it will help?"

"I sure as fuck hope so."

She wanted him. There had been chemistry from minute one, but the intensity of her desire for him now was amazing. She'd never felt anything like it. And she knew it had a lot to do with Christmas cookies and tree farms and the fact that she'd caught him Googling *how to string Christmas lights* on his phone. She also knew it was about falling in love with the little town of Sapphire Falls that had turned out to be all she'd imagined and more.

And it had a lot to do with the realization that they had an expiration date.

This Christmas wonderland wouldn't last. The holiday would end, the snow would melt, Levi would go back to Vegas and she'd go back to San Francisco and all she'd have left was the ornament and her memories. The deadline, the ticking countdown, was also making this all feel so much more bittersweet. It was part of the whole illusion. Like a dream that she knew she had to eventually wake from. She wanted to pack as much as she could into their time together while it lasted.

"Maybe we could—"

"I'm trying to get to a light dove-gray here," he said.

She had no idea what that meant. "What?"

"My cold, black soul is coming back from the dead. I think I'm in the middle-gray tones now versus black. If I can sit on that couch and cuddle with you for an entire movie, I think I can make it a light gray."

She laughed. "Cold, black soul, huh?"

"I was this close to a visit from the Ghost of Christmas Future, I swear."

He had a tiny grin partially curling one corner of his mouth, but she could see that there was some truth behind his words.

"That bad, huh?"

"Let's just say that whatever Christmas movie we decide on, I would appreciate it not be any retelling of *A Christmas Carol*."

She pretended to pout. "I love *Scrooged*."

"Let's put it this way—" He pulled her up more securely against the erection behind his fly. "If I watch one of those, I might not be able to perform later."

She wiggled against him and enjoyed his quick, sharp intake of air. "Oh, we can't have that. I have some Christmas wishes that still need to come true."

"And I'll make them all even better than you imagined," he said, squeezing her ass. "As long as there are no ghosts."

If she hadn't seen the bit of truth in his eyes when he talked about trying to turn his black soul light gray she would have teased him further, and maybe even cajoled him into watching the original *A Christmas Carol*. Or maybe the Muppets version. But he was trying to be a good guy here. The least she could do was let him. For a while.

"How about *Elf*?" she suggested.

"Buddy the Elf?" he asked.

"You know the movie?"

"I've been living in Vegas, not under a rock."

They pulled the tree decorations from the attic, along with three boxes of decorations for the windows, mantel and pretty much every other available space in the house. Phoebe had either inherited a bunch of stuff from family or she was a Christmas hoarder.

The lights went onto the tree with only two start-overs—and Levi only consulted his phone six or seven times and used the F word three or four—and they eagerly covered the branches with ornaments.

However, there were a handful that Kate felt they should leave. One was a *Baby's-First-Christmas* with a photo of Kaelyn, another was an *Our-First-Christmas* ornament, not unlike the one Lauren had showed her. There was no photo, but the date painted on it was the first Christmas Joe and Phoebe would have been married. There were a few others from trips, including their honeymoon, that Kate left in the boxes next to the tree for when Phoebe and Joe got home.

She hoped they hadn't taken anything away from Phoebe and Joe by not letting them decorate the tree this year.

"Damn," Kate said quietly.

"What's wrong?" Again Levi moved in behind her and wrapped her in his arms.

She really liked it there.

"Kaelyn. And Phoebe and Joe. This is their tree. They should decorate it together as a family," she said.

Levi was quiet for a few seconds. Then he said, "You're absolutely right."

Kate sighed. "We screwed up."

"Nope," he said. "We put up a tree for us. And we'll enjoy it tonight and then we'll take it all down in the morning and they can decorate it together another day. We'll tell them we got them the tree as a hospitality gift."

"But the lights…" She stopped right there. He'd done it. It didn't matter that it had clearly frustrated the crap out of him. It was something new to him, but he'd tackled it for her. "And we hauled all this down." She looked up into his eyes. "You'd do that?"

"Of course."

She turned and put her arms around him. "Your soul is so light gray it's almost white."

"Well, worrying about *all* of these people having a perfect Christmas isn't hurting, I'm sure," he agreed with a grin. "But let's not get crazy. I passed white without a chance of going back when I was about sixteen."

"I want to hear these stories."

"Someday. Maybe." He kissed her on the nose.

Someday. That word held so much…promise.

But someday was far beyond Christmas. Far beyond when she was back in the real world in California.

"So next we need a fire, some wine and the movie," she said, keeping her tone light.

"Yes, okay. I'll work on the fire. You find the wine."

"Great." Some space would be nice. At the moment, she was pretty equally torn between the urge to just strip and see what he did and the urge to get in her rental car and speed out of town without a look in the rearview mirror. This Christmas wasn't supposed to be like the others—no heartbreak, no regrets.

The thing was, she was now in too deep to not miss him like crazy when it was over anyway. But she wasn't sure she'd ever be able to work up actual regret about any of this.

Her mind shifted through her thoughts and feelings faster than she could keep up. She went to the fridge, then the cupboards and the pantry but came up empty handed in the wine department.

"All I could find was this jar labeled Booze," she said, coming back into the living room several minutes later. The glass quart jar was full, the top sealed and a big red ribbon around it with a tag that read "Cranberry". That sounded Christmassy.

"Booze sounds good to me," Levi muttered, sitting back on his heels in front of the hearth. He sighed and looked up at her. "The fireplace doesn't work."

"Really? That's weird." She hid her grin. It was not a gas fireplace. There was no on switch. It was clearly a real wood-burning fireplace and it obviously worked. There were blackened logs in it and tools that were clearly not for show.

Kate was willing to bet that Levi hadn't ever lit a real fire in his life. Hell, she only knew it was possible because she'd read about it in books and seen it in movies. It wasn't like the guys she hung out with regularly went around building fires all the time. Nor did any of them have a need to do such a thing.

Levi wasn't the outdoorsy type and she didn't care a bit.

Was Travis Bennett sexy in his work boots and gloves? Sure. But Travis would have been sexy in a burlap bag. It was the guy, not what he wore or did that could push Kate's yum button.

And Levi pushed it. Hard.

Levi was a guy more used to ties than denim, and that was just fine with her. A guy who could fix and build things from scratch with his own two hands was nice. Even sexy in some ways. But she could hire someone to get all of that done.

Give her a guy who could make her laugh, who wanted her to be happy and would do everything he could to make that happen, who could make her tingle right down to her pinky toes and kissed her like he'd never get enough.

She wanted Levi exactly as he was. She didn't think he was perfect, but she was as interested in his imperfections as she was in everything else.

"There are other ways to keep warm." She set the Booze down on the coffee table and went to grab a blanket from the seat of the rocking chair.

"I could call Travis," Levi said. Though he didn't sound thrilled with the idea. "Maybe he could come over. Or he could send Tucker. I'm sure they know how to light a fire."

Kate giggled before she could swallow it. She did refrain from saying, I'm sure they can.

Levi narrowed his eyes anyway.

"Sorry," she said with a grin. "Seriously. It's fine. Don't call anyone. We've got blankets and body heat. And Booze. It's all good."

He was willing to call in another guy to do something he couldn't. That lack of ego to give her what he thought she wanted was amazing. How could she not want him? She couldn't remember another time when someone had been so about *her*. Everything growing up had really been about her mom and, at least so far, Kate had consistently chosen men who were pretty into themselves.

Levi got to his feet. "But it's not perfect."

Kate turned on the TV, got into the Netflix account and pulled up the movie *Elf*. She stopped it on the opening scene and turned to face him. "It's not what we planned. But I'm learning that sometimes the stuff we don't plan *is* perfect."

It took a second, but finally he smiled and she could tell he'd really heard her. "Okay."

"And we'll be plenty warm, because we're not just going to be watching *Elf*."

"We're not?"

"No." She shook her head and took a step closer to him. "We're playing a game."

His eyes darkened slightly and he took a step toward her too. "A game?"

She nodded. "It's called strip *Elf*."

Seven

Levi thought about her answer for all of one second. "I love this game." He came closer to her and Kate had to tip her head back to look up at him.

She laughed. "Want to know the rules?"

"If it results you in fewer clothes, then it doesn't matter."

His voice alone was warming her right up. That low, husky tone made little flares of heat dance along her nerves from head to toe.

"Every time someone in the movie says Santa, I take something off. Every time someone says Christmas, you take something off."

"Kate," Levi said, low and husky and hot.

"Yeah?"

"Push play."

She did.

Within only a few scenes of the movie, they were both down to their underwear and were a third of the way through the jar of cranberry Booze.

Kate didn't know what was in the stuff for sure, but every drink was like swallowing cranberry-flavored liquid fire.

And still she found herself reaching for the jar again and again.

Levi reached over and hit pause on the movie as Santa was again uttered. It was time for Kate's bra to come off.

"What are you doing?" she asked.

They were cuddled together on the couch. Between the blanket around them, the Booze and Levi's hot body, she felt like she was basking in the sun on a beach in Florida. The Booze was probably contributing to her feeling loopy, but she knew that a lot of her warm, fuzzy feelings were about the man next to her.

He shifted so he could see her better, but she tipped over when he moved. He chuckled and put her upright again. "You're down to panties and bra, and I want to be sure I'm paying complete attention when these come off."

Kate was adorable when she was a little drunk and laughing at a goofy Christmas movie.

And drinking hot chocolate.

And looking at Christmas trees.

And decorating Christmas trees.

Levi was certain he'd never used the word adorable in his life, even in his own head, and definitely never in regard to a woman he wanted to sleep with.

But Kate really was.

She'd been sitting next to him, nestled against him as if they'd done this a million times. The way she fit against him felt completely natural and he was actually enjoying cuddling for the first time in his life.

But then she'd started getting naked.

They used the word Santa a lot in this movie. Christmas too. He was in only his boxers and feeling warmer and warmer with each article of clothing that ended up on the floor.

Now things were about to get really good.

When Kate tipped over and giggled, he laughed and grabbed her. He moved her onto his lap, straddling his thighs, facing him. It was much like the position they'd been in last night in the truck.

Was that just last night? That couldn't be right. It felt like they'd been together for a year. In a good way.

"Let's go, Katie. They said Santa." His heart was pounding and his mouth was dry.

You'd think he'd never seen a woman's naked breasts before, the way he was acting.

She held his gaze as she reached behind her. She seemed suddenly completely sober. She unclasped the bra and let it fall down her arms.

He'd felt, tasted and kind-of seen her breasts in the truck, but that was nothing compared to seeing them in full light. They were…perfect. And if he knew nothing else, he knew breasts.

He breathed in and out slowly.

She didn't shy away. She didn't blush. She did nothing but sit and let him look for several long moments.

"Hey, Levi," she finally said softly.

"Yeah?"

"Christmas."

The word that would require him to remove his boxers. It was cheating. It was supposed to be in the movie. He didn't care.

He scooted her back off of his lap and stood swiftly, shedding his boxers.

Her gaze was greedy as she took in the sight of him completely naked and fully erect.

Now she was the one breathing in and out slowly, as if trying to gain some self-control.

"Santa," he said gruffly. "Fucking *Santa*, Kate. Get those panties off."

There was no protest or hesitation from her. Her thumbs went to the top of her panties, her eyes still on his cock. She wiggled her hips and pushed the scrap of silk to the floor, stepping out of them and moving closer to him.

He reached for his pants and pulled three condoms from the pocket, tossing them onto the coffee table.

She reached for her pants and pulled three candy canes from the pocket, tossing them onto the coffee table beside the condoms.

He groaned.

She went to her knees.

"Kate—"

"Shh," she told him. "I dreamed about this last night. It woke me up. I had to give myself an orgasm to get back to sleep."

The breath of air he'd taken jammed in his lungs. Kate had given herself an orgasm last night thinking of him? Right upstairs from where he'd been lying on the couch resisting doing the very same thing thinking of her in the truck, coming apart around his fingers?

She looked up at him from her kneeling position, and Levi bit back a groan. There was very little in the world more erotic than a gorgeous woman on her knees in front of a raging hard-on.

Watching his face, she wrapped her fingers around him.

Pleasure ripped through him. From that one touch. He was probably going to die sometime during this blowjob.

Kate stroked her hand up and down his length, squeezing slightly, running her thumb over the head when at the top and brushing her thumb over his sac when at the base.

She repeated the pattern a few times and Levi's breathing grew more and more ragged. "Kate…"

Without a word or a change in rhythm, she reached for the coffee table and picked up a candy cane. She lifted it to her mouth and pulled the wrapper off with her teeth, continuing to stroke him. Then she bit off the curved top of the cane. As she chewed the peppermint candy, she continued the handjob, increasing her pressure and pace.

Levi couldn't tear his eyes from her. The desire in her eyes was addictive, and as the scent of peppermint drifted up to him, he knew he'd forever get hard when he saw the red-and-white-striped mints at the front entrance of every restaurant he went into.

"Kate—" He tried again. Though it wasn't like he wanted her to stop. But he felt like he should say something. Something like, "I've never felt this way before." Or, "Where have you been all my life?"

He bit the words back though. At least he knew enough to know that a woman would be skeptical about the sincerity of any romantic words said during a handjob.

Still, it was a phenomenal handjob.

And then it got even better.

She swallowed the candy in her mouth, lined the remaining peppermint stick up along his length and leaned in.

His hand instinctively went to her head, sinking his fingers into her silky hair as she took him and the candy into her mouth at the same time.

Mentioning the candy canes last night had probably been the smartest thing he'd ever said in his life.

She sucked and then ran her tongue up and down both lengths. She took both nearly all the way in, sucked lightly, then harder. Levi curled his fingers into her hair. He resisted adding his other hand and taking over the rhythm of his cock sliding in and out of her mouth. Barely.

She was making some very nice noises as she sucked and licked even faster, and Levi didn't care if she wanted to include food in every blowjob she ever gave him from this moment on. The sight and sounds of this woman greedily tonguing and sucking him was something he'd gladly do anything to perpetuate.

But he was nearly at his breaking point.

He was absolutely positive he could get it back up again in a short time if he gave in to his orgasm now, but the first time he went over that cliff with Kate, he wanted to be buried deep, and he wanted her right there with him.

With impressive will power and in one fluid motion, he pulled her mouth off him and pivoted to back her up to the couch. He nudged her down onto the cushions on her back, grabbed her hips to position her and spread her knees.

"My turn," he said gruffly.

She still held the cane in her fingers and he took it from her, sliding it into his mouth, wetting the length with his own tongue. He kept his eyes on hers as he drew the candy around her nipple and then leaned in to suck and lick the hard tip. He repeated it on the other side, then licked the candy cane again and drew the sticky sweetness down her stomach, following the candy trail with his tongue. When he got to her bare mound, he again wet the candy. He slid the cane down over her clit, loving the way she hissed at the contact. The scent of peppermint and aroused woman surrounded him and his whole body clenched with the need to have her. Levi forced himself to go slow though, drawing the candy cane along her cleft, circling her clit and then doing it all again.

Kate's hips arched off the couch and she moaned.

Yes, he wanted lots more of that.

He parted her slick folds, reveling in how wet she was, how ready for him. She wanted him, and the realization of what that really meant grabbed him in the chest. This was more than sex. She could have stayed in San Francisco for sex. She could have any man. She'd come to Sapphire Falls, gone to the bar with high hopes. Hopes for something more than anything she'd had before. She'd taken his arm and walked into that town square with nothing but trust and hope. She'd had no way of knowing what would happen. But she'd trusted him with her Christmas. After a lifetime of disappointing Christmases, she'd let him be a part of this one, this one that she'd so needed to be wonderful.

All of those things were crazy things to be thinking when she was spread out before him like this, but this was more than sex. It was even more than candy cane sex.

This was what he wanted forever.

And he'd known her for a day.

That shot desire so intense through him that he almost tossed the candy cane and plunged into her. He wanted to be a part of her, to get to her like she had gotten to him.

But he also wanted her to get wet whenever she saw the red-and-white-striped mints at the front entrance of every restaurant she went into.

When she saw those mints, he wanted her to turn to him, tell him to grab a handful and take her home.

He really wanted that. He wanted to be the guy with her at every restaurant and the guy who took her home.

He dragged the candy cane through her wetness and circled her clit again before leaning in and licking along the same path. He flicked his tongue over her clit and then sucked, the combined sweetness mind blowing.

"Levi."

He felt her hand in his hair and he increased his pressure on her clit while sliding the candy cane a little ways into her heat.

"*Levi.*"

The cane was tiny compared to what she was going to be taking in a minute, but he knew it was partly how naughty all of this was that was ratcheting her desire higher. He added a finger alongside the candy stick, stretching her and stroking deeper.

She widened her legs and increased her grip on his hair.

"More. I need more."

With his thumb circling her clit and his finger deep, he lifted his head to watch her. She was gorgeous. Her neck arched, her hair spilling over the cushion under her, her breasts hard-tipped and perfect. Her stomach muscles quivered and he felt her inner muscles clenching his finger.

"Oh, no, you're not coming apart like this," he said with a grin, loving that he could drive her to that point.

"But…I want…"

"I know, baby," he said softly. "Katie, open your eyes."

She did, and he made sure she was focused on him as he withdrew his finger and the candy cane and lifted them to his mouth. He slid them onto his tongue and sucked both clean. He didn't have to fake the groan of satisfaction he gave at the taste.

She sucked in a quick breath and seemed to be holding it.

"Most delicious thing I've ever tasted." And it was all her.

He dragged the candy cane through her wetness again and this time lifted it to her mouth.

She parted her lips and his cock hardened further. He slid the candy into her mouth and she closed her lips around it, tasting herself and the peppermint as he drew it back out slowly. Her gaze was locked on his the whole time.

"See what I mean?" he asked gruffly.

"I need you," she said breathlessly.

Yes, she did. He just hoped it was even half as much as he needed her.

He tossed the candy cane toward the fireplace and moved to kneel between her knees on the couch. She spread her knees, welcoming him into the cradle of her hips. He reached blindly for a condom on the coffee table and managed to knock all three to the floor.

Kate reached for them, grabbed one and ripped the package open with her teeth as she had with the candy cane. She rolled it onto him in a practiced motion he was *not* going to think about. Instead, he slid one hand underneath her ass, tilted her pelvis and braced his other hand on the back of the couch.

He slid home a second later.

They both moaned, and he stopped, buried deep, just breathing for a moment.

Kate wrapped her legs around his waist and lifted her hand to one breast, playing with the nipple.

And he had to move.

He pulled out slowly, loving how her muscles tightened, trying to hold on to him. He slid in again, also long and slow, knowing that slow wasn't going to last much longer.

"Harder," she begged.

Yeah, slow was over now.

He thrust again, faster and harder this time, pulling out and plunging back in to the sweetest, tightest, hottest body he'd ever had. She seemed to be drawing him deeper each time he moved, and he found himself taking short, fast strokes as she climbed higher and higher.

He felt his orgasm gathering but he needed her to shatter first.

"You feel amazing," he told her. "I love how you clamp down on me. I could stay buried in you forever. Later, I want you on your hands and knees, spread wide, gorgeous ass in the air so I can take you hard from behind."

His words definitely got a reaction. She arched closer and he felt the response around his cock.

"I want to take you in the shower and in the kitchen and—"

"You said I could ride you in front of the fireplace," she broke in.

His whole body clenched hard. "Yes." He had to clear his throat. "Yes, I did."

"Now."

He stopped moving. "Now?"

"I want that now," she said, nodding.

Her whole body was flushed and he could feel how hot and wet she was. She was close.

And there was nothing he wouldn't give her.

He surprised even himself when he wrapped his arms around her and managed to stand up from the couch still buried deep in her body.

He took the few steps around the coffee table and slowly lowered them to the carpet in front of the fireplace.

"I kind of imagined having a fire when we did this," he said wryly.

"I don't care. I just want on top of you."

Like he was going to argue with that. He rolled onto his back and nearly lost it when she pushed herself up to sitting. He couldn't get any deeper and her body clearly loved it as much as his did. Her inner muscles contracted around him hard.

"Oh, yes," she moaned.

She met his eyes, lifted her hands to her breasts and began to move. She tugged on her nipples as she moved up and down on his length, slowly increasing the speed. She took him deep every time, and Levi had to keep his hands from gripping her thighs too hard as his climax grew steadily closer.

Then she leaned back slightly. Her long hair hung between his legs, brushing over his sac and he was ready to go off.

"Katie, I need you with me," he said through gritted teeth, his hands going to her hips to slow the pace until she was further along.

"Not slower," she told him and moved one of her hands from her breast to her clit.

She circled over the sweet spot and Levi could tell she was indeed, right with him.

He replaced her hand on her nipple with his, tugging and squeezing, and she arched her back as her muscles clamped down hard.

"Yes, yes." And she was there, tumbling over the like-nothing-else peak of her orgasm.

Levi let himself go then, thrusting up into her, fast and hard, long strokes that pulled everything out of him and erupted into a hard orgasm unlike any he could recall.

Eight

They finished the movie, naked, wrapped in a blanket on the couch. They didn't lie completely still. They kissed—long and hot and sweet. They stroked hands over every bit of skin they could reach. They talked and teased—some of it dirty, some not. Kate could feel her heart engaging further and further. He was funny and sweet and romantic and truly enamored with her. She'd never had anyone want her like this, and it seemed that he really did want more than her body. He asked about her favorite cities to visit, her favorite color, if she was allergic to anything, her job and her siblings. They talked about surfing, their love of Indian cuisine, the fact that Kate couldn't cook a bit, the fact that Levi didn't even know if he could cook, their favorite wineries in California, their least favorite shows in Vegas, their favorite museums in DC and their favorite restaurants in New York.

They discovered they had a lot in common as the glow from the Christmas tree grew as the sun dropped and evening fell. Neither bothered to get up and turn on any lights. Kate more than got her wish to have hot sex by Christmas tree light.

In fact, they had three more orgasms each.

He was insatiable.

She was more so.

Kate had never been this horny in her life. The ripples of her climax had barely faded each time before she was thinking about another position. But she also found her mind filled with questions, things she wanted to know about him and the desire to show him her favorite coffee shop in Chicago and her favorite spot on the California coast.

And every time she had a surge of I'm-falling-for-him, she tamped it down with a reality check.

He lived in Vegas. He was a millionaire playboy who had never actually worked a day in his life. He jetted all over the world at the drop of a hat and probably had a girlfriend in every city they'd been talking about all afternoon. She lived in San Francisco and loved her job.

They'd fallen into a comfortable silence after the last orgasm. Levi was running his hand over her hair and she was listening to his heart beat under her ear—and wishing she'd quit thinking things like *I could do this every day for the rest of my life*.

This was all make-believe. It had been twenty-four hours. It felt like more. She felt like she'd known him for years. But the truth was, it had been mere hours. Magical, crazy, just-what-she-needed hours, but still only hours.

Phoebe and Joe would be home tomorrow and all of this would change with that anyway. Then they'd go to the formal the next night. And then it would be over.

"I'm starving," Levi suddenly announced.

Kate's stomach growled in answer.

He laughed. "Let's fix that."

He pulled his jeans on and she wrapped up in the blanket and they headed into the kitchen. But they only stood at the center island for about a minute before Kate said, "We're going to have to go out."

"Which means getting dressed." He didn't seem happy about that idea at all.

Neither was she. "I guess we could go into town and get something at the bar or the diner and bring it back here?" she suggested.

"I have a better idea." He went back in to the living room.

She followed, the blanket trailing behind her.

He typed into his phone. "The bar is the Come Again, right?" he asked.

"I think so."

He typed some more and then lifted the phone to his ear. "Hi, I'd like to order some food for delivery."

He paused, listening.

"Do you think for a thousand-dollar tip you could make an exception?" he asked.

Kate snorted. Just like a millionaire to think he could pay people to do anything he wanted.

"Okay, I appreciate that. I'd like a cheeseburger with everything." He looked at her. "What do you want?"

"They'll deliver?" she asked.

He nodded.

Of course he'd gotten his way. She laughed and said, "I'll have the same."

They showered, together of course, while they waited for the food and then collapsed on the couch, spent from yet another orgasm.

She was most definitely going to be spoiled when she went home. Orgasms, cookies, a guy who would do anything for her. California might have perfect temperatures and the best wine, but she was thinking Vegas had some attraction for her—and she didn't mean the neon lights.

But that was crazy. There was no way she was moving to Vegas.

Probably.

That was farther from the ocean, for one thing. For another…she couldn't come up with a really good *another* except that picking up her life for a guy she'd just met was completely nuts. If any one of her friends were considering the same thing, she would quickly and vehemently talk them out of it.

And besides, Vegas Levi could be a completely different guy from Sapphire Falls Levi. They were both under a little bit of a spell here, no question. The very air in Sapphire Falls seemed to suck a person in and make him or her want to stay, put down roots, have neighborhood potlucks and volunteer for the park-clean-up committee.

Phoebe hadn't been kidding when she'd said that people came to Sapphire Falls and fell in love—with the town and with their soul mates. Kate knew Phoebe's friend Adrianne, of the best cookies ever, had come to town from Chicago. Her husband, Mason, who Kate had met twice with Lauren in DC, was from Sapphire Falls but had left for several years. He'd come home for a simple class reunion and…bam, fallen in love. Joe had come to town from DC. He'd already entertained the idea of staying, but it had been about a different woman than Phoebe. That woman, Nadia, had also come to town and fallen in love—which was why Joe had

had to chase her to Sapphire Falls and how he'd fallen for Phoebe. And then there was Lauren. Lauren had been so against the idea of settling down in Sapphire Falls, she'd actually hatched a plan to uncover all the reasons she *didn't* want to stay. It had backfired. Big time. She was now married to a local boy, pregnant with her first child and the head of several committees, including the Christmas in the Country tour of homes.

So really, she and Levi were just the most recent people to fall victim to the charm and fun of Sapphire Falls.

But it wasn't real.

Except it was real for Phoebe and Joe and Lauren and…

She shook her head. No, she couldn't think that way. People *in* Sapphire Falls, who wanted to live here forever, fell in love and stayed. But she and Levi were both visiting, and once they got outside the city limits, especially if they met up somewhere outside of Sapphire Falls, they'd realize this wasn't some magical soul-mate meeting. It was a Christmas fling.

Levi got up to answer the door for the guy who'd become a delivery driver for the Come Again. Levi gave him cash to cover the food and the thousand-dollar delivery fee he'd promised.

She laughed softly. Yeah, living in the country was definitely not real for Levi. He couldn't live somewhere there wasn't twenty-four-seven food delivery.

They ate and continued chatting about everything and nothing. It was comfortable and nice and even the way he ate his French fries turned her on.

His phone dinged with a text message and he reached for it as he stuffed his last fry into his mouth. He swiped the screen and his face broke into a huge grin. He looked up at her. "I have an early Christmas present for you."

She had just bitten in to her pickle spear. She chewed and wiped her hands on a napkin, butterflies fluttering in her stomach. He'd gotten her a gift? She'd considered trying to find something for him but hadn't decided if it was a good idea and certainly hadn't come up with any great ideas yet.

"You didn't have to do that," she said. But she was thrilled he had.

"Oh, I kind of did. It's a present for me too," he said.

Was it a giant peppermint stick?

Kate couldn't believe her mind went *there* first.

Then she looked at the open candy cane wrapper on the floor between them and she admitted she definitely could believe it.

"Do I have to wait for Christmas?" she asked. *Please say no, please say no.* She wasn't good at waiting. At all.

"I can't keep it to myself until then," Levi said. "Plus, Mason and Lauren will want to talk to you as soon as possible."

She felt her smile fade. She was really confused. "Mason and Lauren?" she asked.

He nodded, grinning widely. "They're going to give you a job."

His words repeated over and over in her head a few times, but she couldn't figure out what they really meant. "What?"

"Mason and Lauren own IAS, the company that Joe works for."

"Yes, I'm aware of that. I've talked with them both professionally in DC."

"So you know what they do."

"They work in the field of agriculture."

"Yes, but their scope is wider than that and growing all the time. Their work in soil and water conservation has been immense in the past year. They're also putting a lot of resources behind alternative energy."

Her mind was spinning. "How do you know all of that?"

"I listen to my brother when he talks," Levi said with a shrug. "And I gave them a huge grant about six months ago for a wind-energy project."

And she was reminded that Levi might come across as a devil-may-care playboy, but he was bright, and while he might spend copious amounts of money on frivolous things, he also had a heart.

She blew out a long breath, choosing her next words carefully. "I'm not sure what that has to do with me."

"I texted Mason, asking if there were any opportunities in the company. He said probably not for me." Levi grinned. "But when I clarified that it was for you, he said hell yes. That's a direct quote." He turned the phone so she could see it.

Sure enough, the display read *"Hell yes"*.

"How do you know how to get a hold of Mason Riley?" she asked. It wasn't the most pressing question on her mind, but it was one she'd like answered.

"I asked Joe."

Well, that was simple. "When did this all happen?"

"When you were shaving your legs." He grinned again. "I didn't notice any spots that weren't completely smooth and sweet by the way."

Yeah, well, she hadn't wanted that to change, and he was already very familiar with every inch, so she'd insisted he give her ten minutes alone in the bathroom to run a razor over her legs again. Just to be sure everything was as smooth as possible for as long as possible.

He'd definitely checked her shave job afterward.

Kate rubbed a hand on her forehead, processing what he'd told her. He'd texted Mason Riley to get her a job—and he had. IAS wanted to hire her.

"You don't want to work for IAS?" Levi asked, his grin finally fading a bit as he realized she wasn't quite as enthusiastic as he was about the text message.

"Mason offered me a job a year ago. Lauren offered me a job eight months ago. I've turned them down twice," she said.

He frowned. "Why?"

"They're based in a small town in Nebraska," she said with a shrug. "There are no oceans here. I have a job I love. I'm from California."

"But now you've been here and you see how great it is," he said.

She laughed. "It has been great. For the past—" she looked at the clock on the wall, "—thirty-two and a half hours. And there have been extenuating circumstances."

He gave her a half grin again. "Those circumstances aren't going anywhere."

She looked at him carefully. "What do you mean? You live in Vegas."

He shook his head. "I'm staying."

Her eyebrows shot up. "In Sapphire Falls?"

"Yes."

"Since when?"

"Since I put my car in the ditch and decided that the way I was living was going to kill me."

She blinked a few times. "You mean, you came here knowing that you planned to stay? This isn't new?"

"It's newly appealing," he said. "But I told Joe I'd spend a year here and clean up my act. Now that I've been here, seen the town, met some of the people, I could see myself staying for good."

She snorted and then laughed out loud. "In the town that shuts down by ten p.m., that has no food delivery, that has one neon sign and that's the open sign at the bar? The town that you've been in for less than forty-eight hours? The place that's biggest excitement is the chili cook-off during the fall festival?"

"There's a chili cook-off?" Levi asked.

"There has to be, don't you think?" she returned. Of course, she didn't know it for sure, but there was no way there *wasn't* a chili cook-off in this town.

Levi sighed. "I like it here. I feel…peaceful. Like good things could happen. Like I could contribute to something here."

"What are you going to do?" she asked. She wasn't trying to be mean, but really? "You own casinos, Levi."

"Well, I could…" He trailed off.

"And I may not want to live here forever, but if you put up a casino in this sweet little town, I *will* come back and kick your ass," she said.

He looked at her, his jaw tight, a determined look in his eyes. "You don't think you'd ever come back for any other reason?"

Her heart hurt at that question. She'd love to come back. She'd love to see every season here. She'd love to see *him* in every season.

"To visit," she said softly. "Maybe."

He seemed to be thinking about that. He didn't look happy. But the next thing she knew, he'd risen from the floor and reached for her hand.

She put her hand in his and let him pull her to her feet. He swung her up into his arms and started for the stairs.

"What are you doing?" she asked. But she knew. And she loved it. Even as she knew she should fight it. More time in his arms, more pleasure at his hands, more of his body would be hard enough to walk away from. But he'd shown her today that sex meant laughing and talking, sharing and exploring the other person physically and emotionally.

She'd never had sex that was as good as sex with Levi Spencer. But she'd also never had someone want to know her, every part of her, like he did.

"I'm making the most of the time we have," he said.

She also knew that he was also going to use all of the intimacy and the pleasure and the trust and the vulnerability between them to try to convince her to stay.

It wasn't going to work. Probably. But it was going to make leaving Sapphire Falls the hardest thing she'd ever done in her life.

Nine

Levi awoke alone.

And he wasn't a bit surprised.

He'd expected it. Which was why he'd kept himself, and Kate, up until almost two a.m. making love, talking, laughing and making love again.

He sighed and turned onto his back.

She'd left.

She wasn't scheduled to leave until the twenty-sixth. She was supposed to be here for the Christmas formal. She was supposed to be here for *Christmas*. It was only the twenty-second.

That meant she was going to spend Christmas alone in California.

And that pissed him off.

He was in love with her. He knew it was impossible, that it didn't make sense, that he might be crazy. But he loved her. He wanted her, in every way, all the time, and the idea that she'd left, chosen to be alone on Christmas after everything they'd done and said, made him mad.

And convinced him that she was falling for him too.

She'd run because she was scared.

He got it.

Pushing himself up, he ran a tired hand over his face. He was going to need to call to see what time her flight was and then get a hold of his pilot. But first, he had to go undecorate the house so that his niece would be able to help her mom and dad deck their own halls.

He came to the bottom of the stairs and stared.

The tree was already undone. The other decorations had been re-boxed as well.

The boxes were stacked to the side of the staircase with a note.

Phoebe and Joe, thanks for letting me stay. We brought the Christmas stuff down from the attic for you but knew you'd want to put everything up as a family. K.

As a family.

Those three words slammed into Levi's gut. He'd agreed that they should take everything down, but he'd had images of helping put it back up. As a family.

Somehow, he suddenly felt like a fifth wheel in his own brother's house.

The living room, the remnants of their dinner and their candy canes had been cleaned up too. The blanket was refolded and the clothes that had been strewn around during *Elf* were folded on the arm of the couch for him.

Hers, of course, were gone.

Levi suddenly wanted to throw something. Or yell. Or swear.

He had never ever had an emotional reaction over a woman he'd slept with. That had been one sign of his cold, black soul. He slept with women who he didn't care about even twelve hours later.

But he could happily say that his soul was healing, because he definitely fucking cared this time.

Having a feeling soul already kind of sucked.

He turned a full circle. He had to find his phone. He needed to know where she was now and if he could head her off during a layover or if he needed to meet her in California.

Where the fuck was it?

He stomped around the living room and then headed for the kitchen.

On the center island, next to the plate of remaining cookies and fudge, sat his phone, two candy canes, a Christmas ornament...and a note.

He pulled in a deep breath, his chest hurting. He didn't want to read the note. But he pathetically wanted to see her handwriting again.

Opening the folded piece of paper, he swallowed hard.

Dear Levi, This was the most magical couple of days. I know it's not real, that we got caught up in everything, but just like a wonderful dream, I'll always remember this as the best Christmas I've ever had. Katie

The ornament she'd left him was a tiny replica of the Sapphire Falls town square, painted in blues, whites and silvers. Everything from their night there was depicted, including teeny tiny reindeer munching hay in one corner.

He read her note again. And four more times after that.

Not real? A wonderful dream? Everything in that square, everything represented in that ornament, was real. Those reindeer had been real. The trees, the hot chocolate, and dammit, the feelings between them, had all been *real*.

He took a deep breath. He'd known last night that's how she felt, and he got it. The whole thing did seem bizarre.

Maybe he should give her some time. Maybe being away from all of this—him—she'd realize that she missed it. Maybe it would all feel *more* real when she was back in the real world.

And maybe she'd forget all about him and Sapphire Falls.

Fuck.

The front door opened and Levi heard his brother's voice, the sound of footsteps and the roller wheels on a suitcase.

Levi took a deep breath and headed in to the living room.

"Welcome home."

"Levi."

Joe grinned at him and Levi realized how nice it was to have someone happy to see him.

"Levi!" Phoebe came in behind Joe, carrying Kaelyn.

Levi reached for the baby who readily came into his arms. "Hi, beautiful," he said, planting a kiss on her chubby cheek.

He helped them get everything into the house and then, at Phoebe's insistence, he settled at the kitchen table while she got Kaelyn something to eat.

Phoebe put Kaelyn in her highchair, swept over to the fridge and retrieved a plastic container of something that she heated in the microwave, stirred, tested and heated for another ten seconds.

The entire time she talked, she told him about how beautiful DC had been all decorated for Christmas, how Kaelyn had slept through the night at her mom's house and how she hoped that carried over to home now, and how she had to still make two salads for the Christmas formal.

"Salads for the formal?" Levi finally interrupted.

"It's potluck."

He looked at her. "What does that mean?"

"We're all bringing food in and everyone will share."

"I know what a potluck is," Levi told her, though he'd never been to one. "Why are you doing a potluck at a formal ball? Isn't that kind of a church-supper thing or a barbecue thing?"

Phoebe laughed. "This is Sapphire Falls. We don't exactly have a catering company that can serve us a formal sit-down dinner. Plus, people here don't mind. It's the first formal. People are just excited to see Lauren's fancy decorations and have the chance to get dressed up and stuff."

Levi thought about that. A fancy sit-down dinner for the people of Sapphire Falls? How hard could that be?

He pulled his phone out and texted his assistant, Cora. She'd investigate the closest companies, the cost of a dinner like that and how much extra it would be to get them to Sapphire Falls with only a day's notice.

"Don't make any salads," Levi told her after Kaelyn was cleaned up and down for her nap.

"Why not? You think I should do a hot dish?" she asked. "I thought of that too, but it's a lot more work."

"I'm bringing a catering company in for a fancy sit-down dinner," Levi said. "How many people?"

Phoebe stared at him. "What did you say?"

"I'm catering the dinner. Well, I'm paying someone to do it."

"For the whole town?"

"Please. We could fit this tiny town on the floor of one of our casinos," Levi teased. "I mean, everyone would have to cuddle, but they would fit. And people here probably don't mind cuddling."

"You can't…that's impossible…that will cost a fortune."

"Good thing I have a fortune."

Joe came into the kitchen and leaned over to kiss Phoebe and then helped himself to coffee.

"Levi is paying for a fancy sit-down dinner for the Christmas formal," Phoebe told him.

Joe leaned back against the counter next to the coffee pot. "That's awesome."

"That's ridiculous. It's too much," Phoebe exclaimed.

Joe laughed. "Levi doesn't understand the words *too much*, babe. Let him do it."

He met Levi's eyes and Levi had a feeling that his brother understood something had happened that made him want to do this for Sapphire Falls.

"Let him…" Phoebe turned back to Levi. "Really?"

"Really. It's all set up. I just need to give Cora a head count."

Phoebe sighed. "I'll call Lauren and get it."

Levi felt a surge of satisfaction. Kate had asked him what he was going to do here and he hadn't known how to answer. She'd meant as a job, he knew, but he wasn't in need of a job. What he did do for the family business could be handled remotely with occasional trips to Vegas or their other sites. The reason for living in Vegas had been all about the parties.

But what was he going to do here? Besides relax, recover and become a better man?

Become an even better man. He could work on community development, marketing for tourism, and he could provide funding for community projects along with continuing to support IAS.

He was fine. He was going to make a home in Sapphire Falls. He was going to adjust to no food delivery and everything shutting down at ten p.m. on the weekdays. It might take a little time, but he'd do it.

Kate was just going to have to accept that.

"I need to go," he said, pushing back from the table and standing.

"Where are you off to?"

"I need to find a gorgeous blonde and convince her I'm not crazy."

Joe nodded. "You're sure that you're not?"

"I am." And he was for maybe the first time ever.

"I assume you're talking about Kate?" Phoebe asked. "Not just some random gorgeous blonde."

"I'm done with random gorgeous blondes," Levi said. "And brunettes, redheads and anything else," he added before they could ask.

"That was fast," Joe said mildly.

"Fast but not crazy," Levi agreed.

"Where is she right now?" Phoebe asked.

"On her way back to San Francisco." He looked at the clock. "She'll be getting to Denver in about thirty minutes."

"San Francisco?" Phoebe asked, clearly alarmed that she hadn't known her friend had left town. "I thought she was downtown getting a pedicure or something. Why is she going home?"

"Because in her life, happiness and fun have always covered other things up. She didn't want to dig down through the happiness and fun here to find out what it was covering."

Joe and Phoebe both looked startled by his insightful answer.

"And what's underneath it here?" Phoebe asked.

"More happiness and fun," Levi said.

Phoebe seemed to like that answer.

Joe, on the other hand, said, "Sapphire Falls isn't perfect, Levi. It's not *all* happiness and fun."

"Yeah, well, good thing Kate's happiness isn't about Sapphire Falls then." Levi started for the door.

"It's about you?" Joe asked.

"Damn right."

"What about your cold, black soul?"

Levi shrugged. "I'm thinking it might be kind of an ecru at this point."

Joe laughed. "I've always thought so. You know, deep down underneath. Way deep down."

Levi grinned and pulled his phone from his pocket.

"Hi, Chris," he greeted his pilot a moment later. "I'm going to need the helicopter. And a way to keep hot cocoa hot. And the biggest candy cane you can find."

Chris didn't hesitate. Requests like this weren't that uncommon from Levi. "Where am I picking you up?" he asked.

"You have coordinates for Joe's house?"

"Yep."

"He's got a pasture. That should work right?"

"Joe's got a pasture?" Chris asked.

Levi laughed. "And a barn."

"Well, this I've got to see."

Layovers sucked.

She had nothing against Denver as a city or even the Denver airport, but she really did hate four hours of sitting around. Because that was four hours where she couldn't throw herself into work or wallow on her couch with Netflix. Which meant it was four hours of thinking…and feeling.

She was so tired of thinking and feeling. She'd been second-guessing leaving. She'd been missing Levi. She'd been regretting not taking photos of Sapphire Falls.

She sighed, slumped down in her chair in the gate area, tipped her head back and closed her eyes.

"I've decided that Sapphire Falls is *more* real than anywhere else on earth, and I thought you should know."

Her head came up so fast at the familiar voice that she felt her neck muscles cramp.

Now she *had* to be dreaming.

Levi stood in front of her in the crowded gate area.

He was carrying a candy cane that was as tall as he was.

"*That* is never going to work," she said, straightening fully.

He gave her a wicked grin and handed her a hot chocolate. It was in a plain white Styrofoam cup with a plain white plastic lid. No way had he gotten this in the airport. Any store here would have their logo stamped all over it.

"What's this?"

"A reminder of how simply this all started," he said.

He'd brought her hot chocolate from Sapphire Falls. Kate swallowed hard and pressed her lips together. When she was pretty sure she wasn't going to sob, she asked, "What are you doing here?"

"I've been thinking about your note."

She winced. She knew it wasn't cool to only leave a note behind.

"And," he went on, "I was watching Joe and Phoebe at home. Feeding their daughter, cleaning up spilled milk, rocking her to sleep, talking about groceries and the formal. And I realized something…Sapphire Falls is as real as it gets. Family, home, love, neighbors, taking care of each other, that's all real. People wanting to have a formal so badly they're willing to do it potluck, that's real. Serving hot chocolate in the town square to raise money for the nursing home residents, that's *real*, Katie." He moved in closer to her.

Neither of them paid any attention to the people around them.

It was just the two of them in this moment.

Kate had to remind herself to breathe.

"You and I don't know real life. We haven't had to struggle financially. Neither of us have parents who would do anything for us. Neither of us have fallen in love. We haven't had a normal Christmas or, probably, a very normal anything else. But Sapphire Falls can teach us about normal and real."

Oh my God. She loved this. She loved everything he was saying. She loved his voice, the earnest look on his face…him.

She probably loved him.

She wasn't quite ready to say that for sure, but…yeah, probably.

"I don't know if I can just pick up and—"

"I know," he said. "I know you can't just move to Sapphire Falls now. I totally get that. And I know that you can't know for sure that you're in love with me yet either."

She wanted to protest. She really did. She wanted to assure him that she *did* love him, that she wanted everything he was saying, but it was too fast, too crazy, too soon.

He went to one knee in front of her and her eyes widened.

He's going to propose! Oh my God.

And in that moment, she knew that she would say yes.

"So take your time," he said. "Take longer to fall in love with me if you need to. That's fine. Just don't stop falling in love with me once Christmas is over."

Kate felt the tears fill her eyes. Her hands flew to cover her mouth.

That was the best thing anyone had ever said to her.

Finally, she nodded, sniffed and lowered her hands. "Okay. I promise not to stop. Maybe ever."

The grin he gave her shot straight through her heart. Like Cupid's arrow.

Wrong holiday, but she liked the idea.

She leaned forward and threw her arms around his neck. "I can't believe you came after me."

He chuckled. "No one can." He gathered her close and stood up. They were pressed together, nose to toes, and he kissed her. It was everything it always had been—hot, sweet, sexy, bold—but there was something else there, something that she finally let herself believe…magic. There was still magic in his kiss and there was no Sapphire Falls air around them, no mistletoe, no cranberry Booze buzzing through her bloodstream.

It was real.

"So let's go to San Francisco," he said, when he finally released her lips.

"You're coming with me?" she asked, pulling back slightly and dashing the tears from her cheeks.

"Of course. There's no way you're spending Christmas without me."

"You'll be there for Christmas?" she asked.

"Every Christmas for the rest of your life if you'll let me," he told her solemnly.

Her heart turned over in her chest. That sounded damn good.

"But I can't move to California right now," he said. "I'm spending a year in Sapphire Falls. I told myself and Joe that I would, and it's time for me to start following through on my good intentions."

"So we'll try a long-distance relationship for a while," she said, trying to sound confident about it. Those were hard. But if the alternative was *not* being with Levi, she'd handle the distance thing.

"Well, yeah," he said with a shrug. "I have a private plane and a helicopter. I can be in San Francisco within a few hours. It won't be a normal long-distance relationship."

She laughed and hugged him again. "We'll work up to the normal-life stuff."

He squeezed her, leaned back and pulled something from his coat pocket. "By the way, you left this behind."

He handed her the Sapphire Falls ornament.

Her eyes misted again. "I tried," she said, taking it from him. "But it really is impossible once you've been there." She knew that he knew she was talking about more than the ornament.

He kissed her again, and when they finally pulled apart, Kate knew exactly what she wanted for Christmas.

"Levi, would you be my date for the Christmas formal in Sapphire Falls?"

It took him only a second to give her a big grin and a, "Hell yeah. And wait until you see what I did for the formal," he said, shouldering her carryon bag and taking her hand.

She laughed. "I'm sure whatever it is, it's perfect and thoughtful and a little out of the ordinary."

Levi didn't protest any of those things.

"And—" he gave her another grin, "Joe taught me how to build a fire in the fireplace while I was waiting for the helicopter."

"But Phoebe and Joe are home now. We can't use their fireplace," Kate said. But wow, did she want to. Her body hummed with the memories of the night before.

"No. But the house I bought has a fireplace too."

"The house you..." She trailed off and shook her head. "We're definitely going to need to work up to the *normal*-life stuff."

The helicopter was waiting for them, prepared to take them on to San Francisco based on Levi's initial plan, but the pilot was happy to take them back to Sapphire Falls instead.

A couple of hours later, they finally flew over the tiny Nebraska town and took in the sight of the town square from the air. It looked so much like the ornament Kate had in her pocket that she sucked in a quick breath.

Levi leaned over and said softly, "You know what that is don't you?" he asked softly. "That's the view of our Christmas future. And not a ghost in sight."

She laughed, but gazing at the brightly lit gazebo, trees and even the hot chocolate stand, she knew it was more than that. She took Levi's hand and squeezed it. "Actually, I think that's simply the view of our future. For all seasons."

About the Author

Erin Nicholas is the author of sexy contemporary romances. Her stories have been described as toe-curling, enchanting, steamy and fun. She loves to write about reluctant heroes, imperfect heroines and happily ever afters. She lives in the Midwest with her husband who only wants to read the sex scenes in her books, her kids who will never read the sex scenes in her books, and family and friends who say they're shocked by the sex scenes in her books (yeah, right!).

You can find Erin at
www.ErinNicholas.com
on Twitter (http://twitter.com/ErinNicholas)
on Facebook (https://www.facebook.com/
ErinNicholasBooks)

LOOK FOR THESE TITLES BY ERIN NICHOLAS
Now Available at all book retailers!

SAPPHIRE FALLS
Getting Out of Hand (book 1)
Getting Worked Up (book 2)
Getting Dirty (book 3)
Getting In the Spirit, Christmas novella

THE BRADFORDS
Just Right (book 1)
Just Like That (book 2)
Just My Type (book 3)
Just the Way I Like It (short story, 3.5)
Just for Fun (book 4)
Just a Kiss (book 5)
Just What I Need: The Epilogue (novella, book 6)

ANYTHING & EVERYTHING
Anything You Want
Everything You've Got

COUNTING ON LOVE
Just Count on Me (prequel)
She's the One
It Takes Two
Best of Three
Going for Four
Up by Five

THE BILLIONAIRE BARGAINS
No Matter What
What Matters Most
All That Matters

SINGLE TITLES
Hotblooded

PROMISE HARBOR WEDDING
Hitched (book four)

BOYS OF FALL
Out of Bounds, Erin Nicholas
Going Long, Cari Quinn
Free Agent, Mari Carr

Enjoy this Excerpt from

GETTING OUT OF HAND

Sapphire Falls, book one

by Erin Nicholas

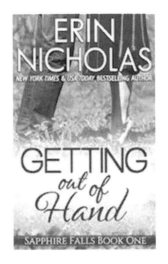

Genius scientist Mason Riley can cure world hunger, impress the media and piss off the Vice President of the United States all before breakfast. But he's not sure he can get through his high school class reunion.

Then he meets the new girl in town.

Adrianne Scott loves Sapphire Falls. The sleepy little town has been the perfect place to escape her fast-paced, high stress lifestyle. Her only plans now include opening her candy shop and living a quiet, drama-free life.

Until Mason Riley bids four hundred dollars just to dance with her.

Mason sure doesn't look—or kiss—like a genius scientist geek. In fact, he makes Adrianne's heart pound like nothing she's ever experienced. Passion like this with a guy who travels the world and parties at the White House should probably be a red flag for a girl who wants a simple boring life.

Good thing no one falls in love in a weekend.

Excerpt

"'Kay all, Adrianne's next."

A hand shot up in front before Jack even asked for a bid.

Jack chuckled and started the action at thirty dollars. It quickly climbed to two dances and fifty dollars.

Adrianne. Mason had no idea who she was, but it was obvious she was damned popular. She was no Hailey Conner, and in Sapphire Falls she never would be, but at least the guys around here hadn't missed the silkiness of the blond waves that fell to her shoulder blades, or the sweetness of her smile, or the perfect curve of her ass—

Mason straightened. What the hell was that? His type was about four years younger than Adrianne, twenty pounds lighter and *not* from Sapphire Falls.

"What's her story?" he asked Drew.

"Adrianne Scott," Drew said with an appreciative sigh. "She's new."

"Yeah. I noticed."

"Been here a couple of years. She's friends with Hailey. Everyone wants her."

He'd noticed that too. And it bugged him.

"She's not dating anyone?"

Drew chuckled and shook his head. "Nope. Not for lack of trying. She never dates. The first guy to kiss her gets a hundred bucks."

Mason raised an eyebrow. He didn't necessarily approve of guys kissing a woman to win money, but then again, he was quite sure that no man would want to kiss Adrianne *just* for money.

"Everyone wants her."

The guys in Sapphire Falls might have more taste than he'd given them credit for.

He drained the beer he didn't want and disliked immensely and decided to place a food order to go. This was all of no interest to him.

"Okay, sixty-five dollars and three dances with Miss Adrianne Scott. Going once—"

Then she laughed at something the woman next to her said.

And Mason was in trouble.

Well, hell.

"Three hundred dollars," he called out.

Every single pair of eyes in the room turned to look at Mason at the same time.

He'd never been the center of attention without a microphone in front of him and a conference logo behind him before. Certainly never in Sapphire Falls.

He stepped forward. He'd opened his big mouth, couldn't really go back now. He should probably be more surprised that he'd bid like that, but he wasn't. He was a genius after all, and while his brain and mouth almost never disconnected, paying a few measly bucks for a chance to dance all night with Adrianne Scott and hear that laugh again was a genius move.

"Did you say three *hundred*?" Jack demanded, pointing a wooden gavel at him as if challenging him to take it back.

"Yes, sir," Mason replied, looking at Adrianne when he added, "For the rest of the dances tonight."

Adrianne's cheeks were pink and her eyes wide. She wore no makeup to enhance the features that were completely captivating him. Her hair was loose and she wore a simple white cotton tank under a denim shirt with blue jeans. Simple, unadorned, and yet he had never been more drawn to a woman.

Jack looked around the room. Obviously, it was unprecedented for a man to monopolize a woman for the entire evening.

"But it's only—" Jack started.

"Four hundred," Mason answered, still watching Adrianne.

"I don't—"

"Maybe we should let the lady decide," Mason interrupted, walking toward Adrianne.

"I can't," she said, shaking her head as he advanced. She was breathing a little fast and she darted her tongue out and wet her bottom lip.

He took another step toward her. "Then what are you worth?"

She swallowed and glanced around. "There's only three dances left," she said. "I can't let you pay three hundred dollars for that."

"I offered four," he reminded her, moving in closer still.

She smiled and he couldn't stop staring at her mouth.

"I meant that even three was too much."

He was directly in front of her now, and only those within about ten feet of them could hear the conversation. "I didn't tell you what I expected those dances to be like for four hundred dollars."

Adrianne was having a hard time breathing. A man hadn't done that to her in a really long time. She liked it and hated it at the same time. She pressed a hand over her heart, which was, not surprisingly, pounding. She took another deep breath. It might be safer to say no. But she made the mistake of looking up into his eyes and knew instantly that she was not going to say no to this man. No matter what he asked of her.

He was something. He wore khakis to everyone else's jeans and a blue button-up shirt instead of a T-shirt. And he moved with purpose and confidence in front of this crowd even though he wasn't one of them. He was tall, his smile was sexy, his voice was sexy—

"How about you loan me that other hundred and I'll bid on you next hour?" Adrianne asked.

He cocked an eyebrow, having noticed her eyes on his mouth. "I'm worth two hundred less than you are?"

She shrugged. "There are ways of finding that out, I suppose," she said without thinking.

Dammit. She was flirting. She didn't do that. Not with guys in Sapphire Falls, for sure. She hadn't flirted in almost two years with anyone.

He gave her a lazy smile that clearly said he was willing to prove anything she asked and Adrianne felt her stomach flip.

She felt his gaze follow every move as she shrugged out of the denim shirt she'd worn unbuttoned over the spaghetti-strapped white tank and tied it around her waist.

"He wins," Adrianne told Jack over her shoulder. "Make it a slow one."

She took the man's hand and led him to the edge of the dance floor while they waited for the other women to be matched with dance partners.

"Is this dance auction a new invention? Because it's an effective fund-raising technique."

"Yeah, it's been part of the festival for the past couple of years. At least it's better than a kissing booth, which was also suggested," Adrianne said, smiling up at him.

He gave her a small smile in return, but his eyes were focused on her lips. Her heart tripped and she pressed her hand against her chest.

"How is dancing better than kissing?" he asked.

His voice sounded a little husky. Which was dumb, because she didn't know him well enough to really know what his voice usually sounded like.

"Um." She rubbed the pads of her first three fingers in a circle on her chest, willing her heart to slow. With a deep breath, she dropped her hand. "A dance lasts longer than a kiss, for one thing."

He leaned in closer, his eyes on hers now. "I think maybe you've been kissing the wrong guys."